THE RISE OF THE SICARIO

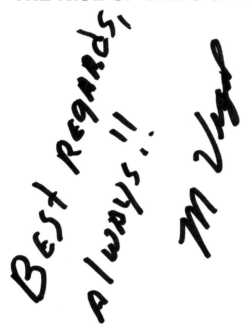

THE RISE OF THE SICARIO

MICHAEL S. VIGIL

THE RISE OF THE SICARIO

iUniverse books may be ordered through booksellers or by contacting:

iUniverse
1663 Liberty Drive
Bloomington, IN 47403
www.iuniverse.com
844-349-9409

ISBN: 978-1-6632-2461-3 (sc)
ISBN: 978-1-6632-2463-7 (hc)
ISBN: 978-1-6632-2462-0 (e)

Print information available on the last page.

iUniverse rev. date: 06/21/2021

FOREWORD

On June 26, 2020, more than two-dozen hit men, known as sicarios in Spanish, set up a series of roadblocks in Mexico City. As Mexico City Police Chief Omar Garcia Harfuch's armored SUV approached, they opened fire. The top cop took three bullets, but survived; two of his bodyguards and a bystander weren't so lucky. The assassination attempt was attributed to the Jalisco New Generation Cartel, or CJNG; Mike Vigil, who served two tours in Mexico with the Drug Enforcement Administration (DEA) called the attack "brazen." "We've had attacks in Mexico City, but nothing like this," Mike said.

Mike knows a lot about attacks, and he knows a lot about sicarios. During his time in Colombia and Mexico with the DEA, he came face to face with sicarios on dozens of occasions. The term sicario became commonplace in Medellin, Colombia, in the 1970s and 1980s, as teenagers were recruited to join the gangs of hired guns who protected the cartel bosses and their operations. The U.S.-led war on drugs, in which Vigil was a key player as a supervising agent in the DEA, included combating these young men, who made a significant contribution to Medellin's homicide rate of roughly 380 per 100,000 people in the early 90s, at the height of the cartel war there. Colombia became the world's most murderous nation. Sicarios are also the primary reason Mexico's homicide rate has skyrocketed over the past three decades and leveled out at about 25 per 100,000 citizens, which security experts deem unacceptably high.

"Don't sweat. Don't let them know you're nervous," that's Mike's best advice for facing down an armed sicario. He stared dozens of sicarios in the face throughout his career. When the gun was pointed at him, "it was critical to my survival that I maintain calm," he says. He learned how to not break into a sweat. "I actually became even more calm in those types of situations because I knew that to break a sweat or become nervous or panicky would lead to my demise."

The first time Mike came across a sicario was in Mexico. Mike was posing as a drug trafficker, and the sicario became suspicious and pointed a gun at him. "I maintained my calm, convinced him I was a legitimate criminal," Mike recalls. "He thought I was maybe a federale, I didn't break a sweat…He finally accepted I was a bona fide drug trafficker." Later, he would arrest him.

As an undercover agent, Mike stared sicarios in the face. But what he rarely got the chance to do was explore the mind and inner life of his enemy. The sicario, in both journalistic and law enforcement lore, is a shadowy figure, one that rarely unmasks itself, one that usually conducts interviews with a deepened voice for effect and protection, one that rarely, if ever, divulges any personal information. Sicario interviews with journalists tend to involve admissions of crimes that are nearly impossible to confirm; any talk of family or friends is usually off-limits, the only serious relationship mentioned by a sicario usually centers around the criminal having found God and forged a new path. The sicario controls the narrative.

In "The Rise of the Sicario," Mike turns the tables, and takes us into the mind of a fictional sicario. Mike draws on his experience with sicarios and knowledge of the criminal underworld in Mexico to paint a portrait of a hit man. Born poor in rural Mexico, Alarico gets his criminal start by stealing avocados with a childhood friend. He and his friend become police officers. They join the Jalisco-based Azteca cartel. He becomes a sicario. He rises through the ranks to become the boss. But he's still a sicario at heart. And the rest is history.

That history, unsurprisingly given Mike's knowledge and insight — which he regularly shares with both the media and law enforcement partners – closely resembles reality. Gone are the days when sicarios were mere henchmen, doing the dirty work for the Mexican drug bosses known as capos. In the modern era of the drug war, sicarios are increasingly reaching the upper echelons of the organizations. The masked thugs of days gone by are, by and large, gone.

Consider Nemesio Oseguera Cervantes, aka El Mencho, who heads the ultra-violent, CJNG. Born to a family of avocado farmers in a rural part of the central state of Michoacán, El Mencho got involved in the drug business as a teenager. After doing prison time on drug charges in the U.S., he was deported at age 30, and joined the Jalisco police force. He earned an honest wage until he apparently realized that operating as a sicario for the local Milenio cartel would be more lucrative and offer him more power. When the cartel split, and the paramilitary group known as Los Zetas moved into Jalisco in the late 00s, El Mencho became a leader of the vigilante group known as the Mata Zetas (Zeta killers). A bloody intra-cartel war, which often drew in the Mexican military, which was trying to quell all violence and establish order — would rage for several years.

This vigilante paramilitary unit would evolve into the CJNG, perhaps the most violent cartel Mexico and the world have ever known. An attempt to capture El Mencho, in 2015, was met with a rocket-propelled grenade attack that brought down a military helicopter. Extreme forms of torture in order to force "ISIS-style confessions," as some media put it, and beheadings have become the rule rather than the exception in CJNG warfare. The assassination attempt of Mexico City Police Chief Harfuch was just the next logical step in the organization's power grab. The U.S. government has placed a $10 million bounty on El Mencho's head, but he remains free.

There is no doubt that the rise of the sicario in the hierarchy of drug trafficking organizations has led to the demise of the gentleman capo of yore, who killed only when necessary, and the ushering in of a new age of ultra-violence, which is not a side effect of the business, but part of the game plan.

Mike witnessed the fall of some legendary gentleman drug lords while in the field as a DEA agent; he can claim credit for investigating and arresting some of the most dangerous among them. He often worked alone in the field, going head-to-head with sicarios without backup. During his last days in the DEA as Chief of International Operations, he witnessed the rise of the global drug cartel, one that can be based in Mexico or Colombia, but benefits from the octopus-like reach of globalization. Now retired in his home state of New Mexico, Mike has witnessed the rise of the sicario, in real life, while writing a fictional account of his own to help document the evolution.

But this time, he leaves the adventure to you, the reader.

Malcolm Beith, February 9, 2021
Beith is a freelance journalist and the author of "The Last Narco: Inside the Hunt for El Chapo, the World's Most Wanted Drug Lord." (Penguin/Grove Press)

DEDICATION

This book is dedicated to the loving memory of my parents, Sam and Alice, whose sacrifice, support and love made me the person I am today.

It is also dedicated to my sisters, Anita and Mona.

To my niece, Ursula, who is my bright shining star.

To Nicole who is in heaven with my parents.

To my stepdaughter, Lisa and my grandchildren, Luke Edward and Sarah Claire.

To my wife, Suzanne, for the stunning book cover.

To my friends, Alvan Romero and Lillie Montoya for their assistance in editing this book.

To my friend, Malcolm Beith, for his touching foreword.

CHAPTER 1

THE BEGINNING

The plush, green colored, rolling hills surrounding Santa Clara del Cobre provided a mystical backdrop to the small town located in the western state of Michoacán, Mexico. The state, with a stretch of coastline along the sky-blue waters of the Pacific Ocean, derived its name from the ancient Nahuatl language used by the Aztecs, which means "place of the fisherman." Rich copper mines have provided most of the town's sustenance for several centuries and even now more than eighty percent of its inhabitants make their living as coppersmiths. As one strolls through the village, the incessant hammering of the orange-colored metal is deafening. The town grudgingly, through time, has clung to its colonial look. Most of the houses and buildings are painted a vibrant white and roofed in ornate red tiles.

Away from the beauty of Santa Clara del Cobre is a much darker side. Several slums lay on the outskirts waiting to be pushed further out with the gradual expansion of the town.

Crime and violence are part of daily life in these decrepit barrios.

Several years earlier, an old, white-haired hag with missing teeth and one greenish eye was assisting a woman in one of the poorest slums give birth to her first child. The old lady was believed to be a bruja (witch) by everyone in the area. They feared her lest she cast a spell on them. The short, stocky woman with heavy indigenous features lay screaming on a bed with her chunky legs spread wide. Her given name was Mercedes Rosales and she was a daughter of the famed Aztec empire, which had been conquered by the Spanish conquistador, Hernan Cortes, in 1521. Despite her noble heritage, she was an outcast and scorned by the lighter skinned population of Mexico. Mercedes had met a handsome man at a "Dia de Muertos" (Day of the Dead) celebration almost two years earlier. She immediately fell in love and a few months later became pregnant. Her vagabond boyfriend, upon hearing the news, quickly disappeared and moved to Mexico City. Mercedes was left to fend for herself. The bruja standing next to a rusty washbasin full of warm water and tattered towels kept telling Mercedes to take deep breaths and push harder so the baby would come out of her womb.

Suddenly, a large, black scorpion with its pincers and curved tail diverted the bruja's attention as it scurried across the dirt floor. At the same time, she heard the loud screech of an eagle nearby.

Startled, the bruja looked down at Mercedes and said, "The appearance of the scorpion and the eagle are a sign your baby will be very special, very special, indeed. Now push harder."

Soon the head of the baby appeared and the bruja with her long, gnarled fingers plucked it out with ease. With a quick swipe of a sharp knife, she deftly severed the umbilical cord. The child was a beautiful baby boy. The bruja swatted his behind and he let out a loud cry. Mercedes and the bruja both noticed the baby had an unusual reddish diamond shaped mark in the middle of his forehead. The bruja told Mercedes the red stood for blood and the diamond shape meant the baby was destined to have wealth. Mercedes smiled broadly as she held her son close to her bosom.

The bruja cackled and placed her hand on the baby's head and proclaimed, "You will go into the world and set it aflame. You will learn hardship and sacrifice, but it will make you stronger. The forces of darkness will protect you as you tread on this cruel and unpredictable universe. You will be a king among kings."

He was baptized Alarico, which meant "power and the ruler of all." Mercedes doted on her child and breast-fed him. He had a voracious appetite. His cradle consisted of an old cardboard box, which Mercedes had lined with a moth-eaten blanket that used to belong to her grandmother.

The horrendous hardships endured by Mercedes didn't

dampen her spirits. She was always cheerful and considered herself blessed to have Alarico who was now her bright light in life. Mercedes baked flour and corn tortillas every morning on her antiquated wooden stove and sold them to customers during the day. People loved them. Mercedes added a secret ingredient to them, which was a little bit of juice from fresh jalapeno peppers.

Alarico grew rapidly into a handsome boy with dark hair and eyes. He loved to play with other children who lived nearby and existed in the same type of squalor. They played tag on the trash filled streets. Skinny, half-starved dogs joined in the melee.

Alarico began school when he was eight years old and began to learn to read and write. Attending school was not very pleasurable for him. He only had one set of clothes, a frayed and torn blue t-shirt and a pair of Levi's that were two sizes too big. On his feet, he had an old pair of Converse sneakers whose soles were beginning to separate from the upper part of the shoes. Mercedes used duct tape to keep them intact. Alarico was embarrassed when pretty girls stared at him on the playground.

In the evenings, Mercedes would prepare Alarico a large bean burrito and every three months she would buy a chicken with money she saved. Alarico counted the days when he could have something more than beans. He savored the simple things in life, which most people took for granted.

After dinner, Mercedes would fill a laminated, round tub with water from a communal facet so Alarico could bathe. She always reminded him of the importance of being clean.

Alarico, at night, would lie on a hard, woven mat and dream of being rich so he could help his mother. He loved her and understood the huge sacrifices she made on his behalf.

At the end of the sixth grade, against his mother's wishes, Alarico dropped out of school so he could help her financially. He could see she was aging rapidly and it pierced his heart. Her hair was turning white and she no longer had the energy to work long hours.

In the evenings, Alarico and his best friend, Samuel, would talk about the hardships of their families. Samuel was the same age as Alarico and was very street smart. He had bushy, brown hair and his eyes were black as coals. He was muscular and a natural athlete.

It was autumn and the weather was beginning to cool. The vegetation was beginning to turn into the bold colors of yellow and gold. The leaves were also starting to fall off the trees and moderate winds swept them across the landscape. One morning, Alarico and Samuel were sitting against a tree discussing ways of making some money.

Samuel commented, "Alarico, last night an idea came to me. Our state is the biggest producer of avocados in Mexico and maybe the whole world. It would be easy for us to steal some. There are some orchards nearby. People love them in their tortas (sandwiches). What do you think?"

"I don't know," replied Alarico. "My mother would be very angry if she knew I was stealing things. It would cause her pain."

Samuel laughed, "My friend, she does not have to know! Besides, winter will soon be here and money will come in handy. Tell her you made it doing manual labor. You have to understand, we are very poor and the government is never going to help us. We are left to survive on our own. Besides your mother desperately needs the money."

"Sadly, you are right," retorted Alarico. "My mother is not well and every centavo will take away from her anxiety. Let's do it then, but we have to be very careful."

Two days later on a dark night, Alarico and Samuel hiked to a large orchard and climbed stealthily over a four-foot, wire fence. The bulky trees were filled with green avocados. Quickly, they filled two burlap sacks with the fruit that was still hard and had not yet ripened.

Suddenly, they stopped and stood still. Voices could be heard of men coming towards them. Alarico and Samuel dragged their bags and hid underneath one of the trees. Soon they saw two men carrying rifles walk by. Petrified with fear, Alarico and Samuel waited a few minutes and then threw their bags over the fence and climbed over. They grabbed their bags and ran for their lives.

Early, the next morning, they stood on a street corner in the middle of Santa Clara del Cobre and began selling their avocados. In minutes, they were sold out and they pocketed a hundred pesos (ten dollars) each. Alarico ran home and handed the money to his beloved mother. She was shocked.

"Alarico, where did you get this money?" asked Mercedes. "Oh, my son, it is a blessing. I haven't been able to sleep worrying about not being able to buy food."

Alarico lied, "I was hired by a rich man in town to dig a flower garden so his wife could plant rose bushes. I think he will give me more work. Let's hope so!"

He felt bad about being untruthful to his mother, but their situation was desperate. He had no other options. Sometimes life forced people to do things they wouldn't normally think of doing. Alarico was just happy he could help his mother and alleviate some of her woes.

Fortunately, for Samuel and Alarico, the avocado growing season in Mexico was yearlong. Every two days, they would steal hundreds of them and sell them for decent money. Their petty crime sustained their families.

One late afternoon, as the sun began to set, Alarico and Samuel walked by an opulent house and watched as a family came out and loaded luggage into a white SUV. Both of them looked at each other and smiled. They waited a few minutes until the vehicle was out of sight and then walked across the street. After checking to see if anyone was watching, Samuel opened a wrought iron gate on the right side of the house. They couldn't believe their luck when they saw a window that was open about three inches. Swiftly, the two friends pushed it up and crawled into the house. In an office towards the back, they began pulling out the drawers from a large desk. Astonished, Samuel and Alarico saw a brick-like wad of money, which they later counted as one hundred thousand pesos (ten thousand dollars). They couldn't believe their eyes. In one of the bedrooms, several handguns, an AR-15 rifle with a sniper scope, ammunition, and a box with numerous pieces of gold jewelry were located. They packed most of the items in several athletic bags stashed in one of the closets. The rifle had a carrying case, which made it easy for them to conceal the long weapon. It was dark by the time they finished ransacking the house. They peeked out the front door and didn't see anyone on the street. It was rather calm other than a few dogs barking in the distance. Calmly, Alarico and Samuel walked out into the street with their loot. They eventually took a small trail through the forest. Half a mile from their barrio, they buried everything stolen from the house and then piled branches on top. They agreed to only use the money that was needed and keep everything else hidden, at least until everything calmed down. The municipal police, undoubtedly, would soon begin an investigation.

Not long after, Alarico became the man of the house and he began to take care of his mother. Every day, he would go to the store and buy her fresh pies, and other pastries. She enjoyed them immensely. It had been years since she had savored anything so good. Alarico felt great joy being able to do things for his mother. She meant everything to him. He adored her.

A few years passed and the health of Mercedes continued to deteriorate. She had also developed a bad case of diabetes, which sapped a lot of her energy. Most days, she stayed in bed and found some relief when sleeping. Alarico would sit in a chair and watch over her. He would make her chicken soup, but she would only take a spoonful. Alarico couldn't help crying, but did it silently so his mother wouldn't hear him. He was having daily bouts of depression.

One day, a group of six soldiers from a military garrison located in the northern part of town came into the impoverished barrio to harass the poor inhabitants. The soldiers, who also came from poverty, now felt superior simply because of their green uniform. They went house-to-house conducting searches and taking anything of value. Many of their victims were punched and kicked. The soldiers took humor in hurting and abusing people. They eventually worked their way to where Mercedes and Alarico lived. A short, dark-skinned soldier smashed the door in with his boot and quickly entered the abode. One of them put the barrel of his AR-15 to Alarico's head and warned him not to move. The other soldiers began searching the small ramshackle house. Mercedes was startled by the noise. Mustering all her strength, she forced herself out of bed and fearlessly confronted the soldiers. She pushed one of them who retaliated and mercilessly hit her on the head with his heavy rifle butt. Blood spurted down her face as she fell to the ground. Alarico, in a blind rage, charged the green clad men. He was punched and kicked until he lost consciousness.

An hour later, Alarico regained his senses and was mortified to find his mother still on the floor in a small pool of thick blood. Quickly, he took her into his arms and carried her to the nearest hospital three kilometers away. After examining her, one of the doctors told Alarico she had sustained a concussion and severe brain damage. He stated the next few days would be critical and assured Alarico they would do everything in their power to save her. Alarico never left his mother's bedside and held her hand.

Three days passed and early one morning, the loud beeping of the heart monitor attached to his mother startled him. Doctors and nurses rushed into the room and began resuscitation measures. A minute later, Mercedes opened her eyes and smiled at her son one last time. She turned her head and allowed death to bring her eternal peace. Alarico buried his mother the following day after a short, heartwarming ceremony by Father Javier Gutierrez, the barrio priest.

For days, Alarico mourned the passing of his beloved mother. He visited the local cemetery every day and placed a red rose on top of her grave. His deep sorrow soon took a darker side, a deep desire for vengeance. He began to obsess about killing the vile soldiers who took his mother's life. In his raging mind, he began to conceive diabolical plans to end their miserable existence.

A strong wind began to whip the air into a frenzy as Alarico and Samuel made their way to the isolated area where they had buried the weapons, money, and valuables. The two men retrieved the AR-15 with the telescopic sights. They had practiced firing the weapons every chance they got and had become very proficient in their use.

Nightfall was beginning to envelop Santa Clara del Cobre as they made their way to a hill above the small military base. The tall grass and cottonwood trees provided excellent cover. While getting settled, Alarico observed soldiers yelling and carrying on as they left the front gate. It was two of the men who had been involved in his mother's killing. He recognized them immediately. Alarico was barely loading the rifle and did not have time to fire at them. The soldiers soon entered a hole-in-the-wall cantina that sold cheap tequila. Mariachi music began to blare from the establishment. Soon, local prostitutes began to arrive in their short, tight miniskirts and semi-unbuttoned blouses, which highlighted their physical attributes. The music got louder. Ominous clouds moved rapidly in the sky towards the Pacific Ocean.

Alarico and Samuel were starting to feel uncomfortable

sitting on the moist ground when suddenly the two soldiers staggered out of the rickety cantina. They were singing loudly causing two street dogs nearby to begin howling and then snarl at the drunken soldiers. Alarico slowly raised his weapon and placed the butt snuggly into his shoulder. He looked into the scope until the crosshairs were centered on one of the unsteady soldiers. He carefully placed his index finger on the trigger. He pulled it gently until a loud blast cut into the night air. The projectile traveling at over three thousand feet per second smashed with considerable force through the rib cage of one of the soldiers. It flipped him backwards into the air and his body spewed blood like a leaky faucet. He was dead in seconds. His comrade's first thought was that he had passed out from all the alcohol. He had not heard the gunshot. He bent over to pick up his friend and that is when he saw all the blood. A split second later a bullet pierced the top of his head. It popped like an overinflated balloon. Alarico felt an inhuman sense of pleasure. The transformation from a poor, innocent boy to a heartless killer was now complete.

Two days later, Alarico and Samuel were back on the hill watching the military base, but were unable to see any of the other four targets. Three days passed and early one morning, Alarico saw the four men walk out with their rifles at the ready. Obviously, they were going out on patrol. Alarico and Samuel ran down the hill and began stalking the men through the quiet streets. When the soldiers turned down an alley, Alarico and his friend quickly closed the distance. They both pulled their handguns and shot the soldiers in the back of their heads blowing out their brains onto the street. Alarico stood over them for a moment and grinned from ear to ear. Vengeance was more intoxicating than the most expensive tequila.

CHAPTER 2

THE ODYSSEY IN AMERICA

It was a bright, sunny day and Alarico and Samuel were sitting on a wooden pew inside the beautiful parish church near the middle of town. It was one of their favorite places. They loved looking at the ornate copper chandeliers and wall decorations that adorned it, but more so enjoyed the peace and tranquility it provided. Their conversation was centered on embarking on some exciting adventure.

Alarico stated, "Samuel, we need to look at expanding our horizons. We can't be like most of the people here who live and die without knowing what exists outside of Santa Clara del Cobre. They live in a cocoon and are afraid of the unknown. We are better than that, don't you think?"

"Of course, it would be a sin not to explore the world and learn from those experiences," replied Samuel. "What do you have in mind?"

Alarico smiled, "I would like to go to America. It is known as the land of opportunity and who knows we may find our fortune there. The U.S. government does a lot for its people while ours only steals from us. What do you say?"

"How do we get there since we have no papers?" inquired Samuel. "We are poor and could never get a visa to travel there. They only give them to people who have money."

Alarico chuckled, "Not to worry! I know a coyote (alien smuggler) who will help us. His name is Federico and he is always smuggling small caravans of people from Central America into the U.S. I will contact him tomorrow morning."

The next afternoon, Alarico walked five miles to a small, isolated ranch, which had a red barn in the back of an old house with a wraparound porch. He found Federico sitting in front on a rocking chair with a toothpick in his mouth. He was a tall, slender man who sported a crew cut. He looked more like a soldier than a smuggler of aliens.

"Federico, how are you?" yelled Alarico. "I am so glad my long walk was not in vain. I came to see you about smuggling me and my friend, Samuel, into the U.S."

Federico grunted, "Are you sure? It is not all peaches and cream there, my friend. There is much discrimination in that country and if you get caught without papers, they will either deport or throw you in prison. The U.S. Border Patrol and Immigration officials are a bunch of racist cabrones."

"We know the risks, but are willing to take them," retorted Alarico. "Besides, if we don't like it there, we can always come back to Mexico. Will you help us?"

Federico smirked, "Okay, if that is what you truly want? I am taking a group of thirty men, women, and children from El Salvador to the border with California in four days. Can you be ready by then?"

"I can assure you we will be ready," replied Alarico. "How much will you charge us for your service? Keep in mind, we do not have a lot of money."

Federico laughed at the comment, "Keep your money! You will need it to survive where you are going. Also, just bring a few clothes. We need to move fast once we cross the border. Be here in four days in the early morning hours."

Alarico thanked Federico and then jogged back home through a heavily wooded area. Later, he met with Samuel and told him the great news. Samuel expressed concern about having enough money to sustain them until they were able to find jobs. The next day, Samuel arrived at Alarico's house with a proposal.

Samuel frowned, "Listen, if we are going to the U.S., we are going to need some money. We have almost used all the money we stole so we need to have something to fall back on. I have a cousin who is a small-time drug dealer and we can buy a pound of heroin from him at a great price. We can sell it across the border for a lot of money."

"I don't know about that," answered Alarico. "If we get caught, they will send us to prison. Also, we don't know anything about dealing drugs. Who would we sell it to? We can't just approach people on the street and ask them if they want to buy it."

Samuel countered, "It will take us very little time to find customers. A lot of people use drugs in America. They are fucking zombies. We will be extra careful."

"I guess we really don't have a lot of options," lamented Alarico. "We just have to be cautious and not make any mistakes."

The following day, Samuel dug up the money he and Alarico had buried and went to see his cousin who sold heroin for one of the cartels. Samuel handed him a wad of money and grabbed the pound of heroin, which was in a large, clear plastic baggie. The lethal powder was brown in color and smelled like vinegar.

A few days later, Alarico and Samuel, each carrying a small bundle of clothes inside plastic bags they had saved from purchases at a local grocery store, walked rapidly to Federico's house. The sun had not yet risen and the darkness gave them a sense of trepidation. When they arrived, they saw a large group of people in worn and tattered clothes clustered together. They looked malnourished and a deep sadness was etched on their faces. A few of the children, clutching their mothers, cried loudly. Parked nearby was an old, red tractor-trailer truck. Out of the corner of his eye, Alarico spied Federico approaching from the side of the house.

"Alarico, I was not sure you were going to come," laughed Federico. "And who is your friend?"

"This is my best friend, Samuel," replied Alarico. "I had mentioned he would be coming with me. It looks like you have a full load of people."

With a serious demeanor, Federico stated, "Yes, all of them arrived yesterday and they are anxious to begin the long journey. Most of them are fortunate to have family members in the U.S. who will provide shelter and help them financially."

In a very loud and authoritative yell, Federico ordered everyone into the trailer. It didn't have air conditioning and was painfully hot. Packed like sardines, people began to fan themselves with pieces of cardboard and some with the baseball caps they wore. Alarico and Samuel sat together, but were extremely uncomfortable. A minute later, several men began stacking large boxes of avocados into the big rig to conceal the people inside. This made it even hotter. People began to sweat profusely. The fanning was now at a fever pitch as desperation began to set in, but it was too late for anyone to get off the vehicle.

There was a loud shudder and the clamorous sound of gears grinding as the tractor-trailer began to move forward. It headed north. Twelve hours later, the vehicle arrived in Culiacan, the capital city of Sinaloa. The rig took a three-mile detour on an isolated dirt road and then stopped abruptly.

Two men took out dozens of boxes of avocado's allowing the migrants to exit so they could stretch their legs. It was a warm day, but to the half-baked and half-crazed group the fresh air felt like the blast of an arctic wind. They desperately gasped for air and some vomited on the ground. They felt miserable and still had several more hours to go before they arrived at their destination. Federico and his men handed out bottled water and cheap, cold cut sandwiches with a dab of stale mustard. A dog would have turned his nose at the food, but the migrants were starved. Alarico and Samuel took a single bite and gave them to a woman with two children. She smiled and thanked them profusely.

After half an hour, everyone crawled back into the trailer with a little bit more energy. Alarico suddenly began to sing and was soon joined by several others. It helped keep their spirits up. One song led to another. Everyone was off key, but the ensuing laughter was heartwarming and refreshing.

On the southern outskirts of Ciudad Obregon, Sonora, the federal police had put up a roadblock. They were looking for illegal drugs. Several men carrying AK-47s were searching a long line of cars and trucks. They looked mean and focused. Federico rolled down his window.

"What do you have in the truck?" asked one of the federales. "I notice you have license plates from the state of Michoacán."

Federico calmly answered, "We are transporting a load of avocados to the border where they will be sold to the gringos."

"Open the doors to the truck so I can take a look for myself," retorted the officer. "If you have nothing to hide, I will let you continue on your way."

Federico opened the driver's door and jumped down, but stepped on a large rock and lost his balance. He fell hard on the asphalt and almost broke his nose. The federale roared in laughter. With all of the dignity he could muster, Federico stood up and felt his sore nose, which was full of abrasions. In pain, he made his way to the back of the trailer and opened the large metal doors. The federale took out a box and examined the avocados.

He said, "Chingado, I am not going to spend all day offloading your truck. I don't have the energy in this heat. You are free to go, but I am keeping this box for my family. Now get the fuck out of here!"

Federico smiled and got back in the truck. He gave a friendly wave to the federales and accelerated down the narrow road. In another four hours, they arrived in the border city of Tijuana, Baja California Norte. Night was starting to settle in and traffic on the streets began to diminish. Federico drove into a large warehouse fifty meters from the U.S. border. Several men who were waiting quickly unloaded the boxes of avocados and allowed their human cargo to escape from their confined space.

Inside the warehouse was the entrance to a sophisticated tunnel, which was hidden underneath a large billiards table with a hydraulic system. One of Federico's men pushed a button on a corner of the table causing one side to lift high in the air.

Federico addressed the migrants, "You will be smuggled under the border to the southern section of San Diego, California. The area is known as Otay Mesa, which is full of warehouses and therefore is an ideal place for us. Don't be scared of going through the tunnel. It has great ventilation and lighting. You will be totally safe. You will come out at another warehouse where I have several men and vans to drive you to different bus stations. They will help you buy tickets to wherever you want to go in the country."

A short, dark-skinned man with ragged clothes asked, "What if we don't have any family in America?"

"That will not be a problem," responded Federico. "There are hundreds of farms in California where you can find work picking crops like lettuce, strawberries, and oranges. A cousin of mine has hundreds of orange groves and he is always looking for workers. It will be an advantage to many of you because it will allow you to get accustomed to America. Later, you can spread your wings and move someplace else with better job opportunities. Alright, let's get moving!"

The migrants, in a single file, began climbing down a long wooden ladder into the tunnel, which was thirty feet below the earth. Mothers and fathers quietly helped their children so they would not fall. Even though the tunnel was ventilated it had a musty smell. The tunnel was five feet six inches high and three feet wide. Everyone was scared since they had never been in one before. They feared it would collapse and they would be buried alive. Women had tears streaming down their cheeks and several children began to scream. Alarico, Samuel, and Federico were the last ones to enter. They walked half a mile and then climbed another wooden ladder into a large, metal warehouse littered with wooden pallets and assorted junk. Several burly men stood in front of six large vans with dark tinted windows preventing anyone from seeing inside. All of the migrants, with the exception of Alarico and Samuel, jumped into the vehicles, which quickly left the warehouse.

Federico told the two friends, "I know that you don't have much money right now and I can take you to Logan Heights, which is nearby. You will fit in since it is mostly a Mexican community. It is a poor barrio, but for now it will work for you. What do you think?"

"What the hell, we have nothing to lose," commented Alarico. "Do you know of very cheap apartments we can rent and where they will not ask a lot of questions?"

Federico laughed, "I know San Diego like the back of my hand. I am aware of several that are very cheap and as long as you pay your rent on time they could care less if you were Osama Bin Laden. Let's go!"

They walked to a beat-up, gray Ford panel truck, which was parked outside. The doors creaked loudly when they opened them and the upholstery on the seats looked like they had been slashed with a sharp machete. There were no seat belts, but off they went.

In less than an hour, the trio arrived in Logan Heights. Alarico was surprised at how the area resembled many parts of Mexico. Most of the people on the streets were of Mexican descent. Many of the houses were old and in need of repairs. They drove through Chicano Park, which displayed an amazing number of murals and unusual sculptures. Soon they arrived at a small, skid row apartment complex.

Alarico remarked, "It can't be any worse than the shack I grew up in. Actually, it is a step up from what I am used to."

The three men went into the dingy office where a heavily wrinkled, older woman looked up and smiled as they entered. After learning Alarico and Samuel wanted to rent an apartment she grinned and stated a one bedroom, with a bathroom and small kitchen was three hundred dollars a month. It was to be paid in advance. She also accepted pesos. She took the men to a second story apartment, which sorely needed paint. A large rat with a lacerated tail scurried out the door, down the stairs, and ran into a large bush. The interior of the horrendous dwelling smelled of stale cigarettes and cheap booze. It had a bed with a urine-stained mattress and the carpet had the stink of mildew. It would have turned the stomach of most people, but Alarico and Samuel were used to poverty and hardships. They took the uninhabitable abode and paid a month's rent.

During the day, Alarico and Samuel walked the streets of Logan Heights to familiarize themselves with the community. They saw the faces of despair on the homeless and the expressions of rage in the hordes of gang members prowling throughout the area. Just about every street corner had drug pushers selling dime (ten dollar) bags of drugs. After befriending several of the young drug dealers, Alarico and Samuel were taught how to dilute the pound of heroin they had smuggled into the U.S. They mixed it with lactose (milk sugar) lowering the purity to street level quality, but quadrupled its quantity. Alarico and Samuel also learned how to package it in small pieces of tin foil for street use. Like all the other dealers they sold each dosage unit for ten dollars. The two friends soon began to make good money on a daily basis.

One morning, Alarico and Samuel were selling heroin in front of their apartment complex when a tall, Hispanic man wearing a black hoody approached and told Samuel he wanted to buy an ounce of heroin. He flashed a wad of crisp, new twenty-dollar bills. Samuel told him to come back in an hour since he did not have that much with him.

Alarico expressed concern, "Samuel, I think that man is

a policeman. Who else would be carrying brand new bills? All of the buyers have old, wrinkled bills. Don't sell to him!"

"My friend, you are like an old woman that worries about everything," replied Samuel. "Besides, we need the money. Let me run and get the ounce this man wants. I will be right back."

Samuel trotted off while Alarico waited. Less than ten minutes later, he returned and was out of breath. Alarico was quiet and was not at all happy with his friend's decision. Soon, the buyer returned and asked Samuel if he had the quantity of heroin he had requested. Samuel nodded and pulled it out of his right pants pocket. It was contained in a small cellophane bag. He handed it to the tall man who put it close to his nose and smelled it. After doing so, he pulled the hood off his head. Suddenly, the squeal of tires could be heard as two unmarked police cars came up the street and several men jumped out brandishing handguns. They grabbed Alarico and Samuel by their necks and slammed them to the ground.

A bald, stocky man with steel blue eyes barked out orders, "You fucking assholes better not move otherwise it will give me great pleasure to put a bullet in each one of you. Do you morons understand?"

Alarico and Samuel remained quiet as they were handcuffed and unceremoniously thrown into the back seat of one of the police cars. They glanced at each other as if to signal each other not to say anything. At the San Diego

Police Department, Alarico and Samuel were processed. Photographs, fingerprints, and personal information were taken from both of them. Afterwards, they were placed in separate interview rooms. Each room consisted of a small table and a few chairs. They were allowed to sit alone for an hour to escalate their anxiety and tension before being questioned. Police officers eventually entered the room, but left disappointed. Alarico and Samuel snubbed their noses at them. Enraged, two of the police officers returned to put them in adjoining cells. Inside the cells they beat Alarico and Samuel on their heads and body with long, black wooden batons. One of the blows smashed Samuel's nose and blood splattered on the walls and floors. He shrieked in pain. After what seemed like a lifetime, the beatings stopped and Alarico and Samuel were left in crumpled heaps on the floor.

Early the following morning, they were escorted to a shower area and given small bars of soap and told to wash the blood off their hair and faces. A short stocky guard then gave each one an orange jumpsuit, which had the word inmate stenciled on the back in black letters. After they dressed, handcuffs were tightly clamped on their wrists. Alarico and Samuel were confused and very apprehensive about their fate. Several guards marched them to a bank of elevators and took them to the basement of the jail where a van waited. They were placed in the back of the vehicle and then driven to a large courthouse in downtown San Diego. Inside a large courtroom, they were told to sit at a long, rectangular wooden table where they waited with tremendous anxiety. They were completely startled when two large doors opened loudly and a black robed judge with white hair entered and sat at a huge desk looking down on them. It was extremely intimidating.

The judge looked sternly at Alarico and Samuel for a few seconds, which increased their fear even more. The judge, using a translator, read them their constitutional rights and the charges against them, which included distribution of heroin and one conspiracy count. He asked them if they had the capability of hiring an attorney. Both quickly answered they didn't have any money and were completely broke. The judge stated that the government would provide a public defender to represent them. A minute later, the two friends were whisked away back to their jail cells.

The next morning, a beautiful, young Hispanic female with dark hair and fair skin came to visit Alarico and Samuel in jail. She introduced herself as Ursula Atencio and informed them she was from the Public Defender's Office.

Ursula, speaking fluent Spanish, commented, "I have reviewed your case and it is pretty clear you willingly sold heroin to a local police officer. The evidence is very strong since Samuel did a hand-to-hand transaction with him. Alarico, you were there when the deal was being discussed and you did nothing to withdraw or voice an objection. If you decide to fight the case in court and get convicted you will receive more time than if you throw yourself at the mercy of the court. Do you understand?"

Alarico responded, "If we plead guilty how much time are we looking at? We have never been in prison before. What can you do for us?"

Ursula smiled, "I am very good at negotiating deals with the district attorney's office. At the moment, they are swamped with cases and therefore more prone to cut a deal. Also, to your advantage is that you have no criminal record in the U.S."

"Well, you are the expert in these matters," replied Alarico. "Go ahead and see what kind of a deal you can get for us and we can go from there. We just don't want to rot in prison."

Ursula retorted, "Fair enough! I will probably get back to you in two days after I confer with the prosecutor handling your case. At that point in time, you will have to decide how you want to proceed."

With Ursula's departure, Alarico and Samuel were thrown back into their dingy cells. Alarico lay on his bunk and stared at the ceiling pensively. He realized fate was teaching them a hard lesson in life. He came to the conclusion they had to become much smarter and more cunning. They could not act on impulses, but had to be more strategic in their thinking.

As promised, Ursula returned two days later. Alarico and Samuel held their breath hoping for good news.

Ursula advised, "Well, the prosecutor is willing to agree

to the following. He will grant you a lenient sentence of three years, but two years will be suspended after you serve a year. In reality, you are getting a sweetheart deal. What do you say?"

Alarico turned to Samuel and they whispered for a couple of minutes. They weighed their options and finally reached an agreement. Samuel had a sad look on his face.

Alarico spoke, "We both accept the deal, not that we have much wiggle room. A year is better than the ten to twenty years we were facing. Thank you for all your efforts on our behalf."

The following week, the two friends appeared in court. The judge asked both the prosecutor and public defender if an agreement had been reached and almost in unison they answered in the affirmative. The judge asked Alarico and Samuel to stand as he pronounced a three-year sentence, but added that two years would be suspended. They were to serve their time at the infamous San Quentin Prison located in California.

CHAPTER 3

THE DEVIL'S HOUSE

A gray prison bus transported Alarico, Samuel, and many other prisoners to their new home, the forbidding San Quentin Prison, one of California's most notorious and violent correctional facilities. The institution was located just north of San Francisco and was the only prison in the state that housed death row inmates. Executions there were initially carried out in a symmetrical metal gas chamber, but since the mid-1960's it shifted to lethal injection, a more humane process.

As they got closer to the prison, Alarico and Samuel saw the massive buildings that would be their home for twelve months. The institution was next to the murky, swirling waters of San Francisco Bay. The two friends were lost in the moment and little did they know their lives would take a drastic detour into a darker and more sinister world.

All of the prisoners were herded into the building in a single file where prison staff provided them with traditional blue uniforms they would wear each day of their incarceration. One of the supervisory guards, a short blond-haired man, met with the sullen prisoners in a large austere room with long wooden benches. Accompanying him was a tall, Hispanic female with short black hair who was the Spanish interpreter. The male guard introduced himself as Bill and the interpreter as Monica.

Bill stated, "Gentlemen, welcome to San Quentin Prison. This will be your place of residence for whatever time you were given and if you stay out of trouble, you may even leave sooner depending on the parole board. The facility was built to house slightly more than three thousand inmates, but due to overcrowding, we now have over three thousand seven hundred inmates. Before you go to your cells, we will pass out copies of our rules and regulations. Make sure you familiarize yourselves with each and every one. If you violate them, you will be punished and ignorance of the rules will not be considered."

Monica then translated in perfect Spanish for those who didn't speak English and added the prison had several violent gangs, which were extremely predatory and warned them to stay away since they were trouble.

Minutes later, the inmates walked slowly in front of several stern looking armed guards to their assigned small cells, each housing two men. Alarico and Samuel were placed into the same cell, which had bunk beds, a steel toilet, washbasin, and a rustic bookshelf on the wall. When they heard the loud clanking sound of the heavy steel door closing behind them, reality hit like a kick to the groin. Both felt a choking, nauseating feeling of claustrophobia and tremendous anxiety. They sat quietly and looked at each other with great sadness.

Alarico spoke in a low voice, "Samuel, we are like brothers and have to take care of each other. I listened to the interpreter and it appears there are many gangs in this prison. We are very vulnerable since we are new. Some of these gangs will soon come calling. We cannot act weak or they will quickly take advantage of us. We have to fight. There is no other choice."

The very next day, the prisoners were let out into the yard to lift weights, play basketball, or just sit around basking in the warm sun. Alarico and Samuel saw groups of scary, tattooed men walking methodically around the area. They were muscled thieves, murderers, and drug dealers. They soon broke off into their respective gangs and watched each other with suspicion. Within minutes, a tall, black man with a jagged scar on his right cheek approached Alarico and Samuel with a sinister look on his face. He proclaimed that he was claiming both of them as his personal girlfriends. They didn't understand him until he tried to kiss Samuel. Reacting quickly, they punched him in the face and kicked him in the right knee. The black convict howled in pain and fell on the ground. Alarico kicked him in the face and the blow knocked out his front teeth. The convict lost consciousness with his face completely covered in blood. Whistles sounded everywhere, and two men motioned Alarico and Samuel over to a concrete table where they were sitting. By the time the guards got to where the convict was lying on the concrete, Alarico and Samuel had blended in with their newfound friends, the Mexican Mafia.

The guards picked up the injured convict, a member of the Black Guerrilla Family, and carried him to the prison hospital.

One of the men introduced himself as Arturo Enriquez. He was a short, dark-skinned man who was the top shot caller for the Mexican Mafia. He hailed from Los Angeles and was serving a life sentence for ordering the murder of three rival gang members. Enriquez had avoided the death penalty in a plea agreement with the district attorney.

Enriquez commented in Spanish, "You vatos (guys) are something else. I like the way you gave that cabron (bastard) a chinga (beating). Where are you from?"

"We are from Mexico and are here for heroin trafficking," replied Alarico.

Enriquez smiled, "If you need anything from me or my camarades (Mexican Mafia members) let me know. You have balls and that is important here."

It didn't take long for Alarico and Samuel to realize that the various gangs, aligned by race, literally controlled the prison on the inside. The gangs consisted of the Mexican Mafia (La Eme), Nuestra Familia, Black Guerrilla Family, and the Aryan Brotherhood. All were hyper-violent and lived by informal codes, which were enforced by extreme violence. The leaders had the power of life and death in the animalistic culture. An order to kill was called a "green light" and whoever was chosen as the assassin had to do it without flinching otherwise, he would quickly become the victim. The prison environment was like an unstable explosive that could go off without needing a fuse or a blasting cap.

Despite stringent security measures, the inmates were able to smuggle drugs and even cell phones into the prison. They created shivs (knives) out of pieces of metal from workshops and even toothbrushes. They used the most secure place to hide the weapons, their rectum. With cell phones, they came up with another ingenious idea. They hollowed out bars of soap and secreted the phones inside and stuffed them in their rectums. It was virtually a bazaar for the criminally insane.

A week later, Alarico and Samuel were in the yard and they felt it was eerily too quiet. Suddenly, without warning, several Nuestra Familia gang members surrounded a bald, white man who was heavily tattooed with Nazi swastikas and SS symbols. They stabbed him with lightening thrusts to the chest and neck. He fought desperately, but within seconds, his carotid artery was severed and dark, red blood spurted out with great force. He dropped to his knees before falling face first to the ground. The sound of explosive gunshots could be heard as guards fired near the inmates to get them to scatter. It was later determined the dead Aryan Brotherhood member had insulted one of the main leaders of the Nuestra Familia in the mess hall by calling him a "greaser." It proved to be a fatal mistake.

To pass the time, Alarico and Samuel began taking English classes in prison. They enjoyed every moment spent away from their cell. Both showed a great aptitude for languages. The two friends studied and practiced speaking the language together and rapidly learned to speak, read, write, and listen in rudimentary English. Every day, they checked out books from the prison library and read in their cells until the lights were turned off. It took several weeks for them to become even more proficient.

The infestation of predators in the prison was overwhelming and it was becoming impossible for Alarico and Samuel to fight them off. They kept coming like an endless swarm of locusts.

One day in the yard, Alarico and Samuel met up with Enriquez who was surrounded by at least ten men wearing shorts and no shirts. They all had the black-hand tattoo on their chest. They suspiciously scanned the area for any potential attack from a rival gang. Paranoia was a normal thing in prison and one could not become complacent.

Enriquez greeted his acquaintances, "Òrale! How are you

doing? I have not seen you in a while. You have not been trying to avoid us, have you?"

Alarico smiled, "No! Of course not! We are just trying to stay out of trouble, but some of these pinchè cabrones will not leave us alone."

"Well, you have the option of joining La Eme and becoming a carnal," advised Enriquez. "This way you would be protected. No one would bother you. What you have to understand is that in prison one has to belong to a gang. You will not survive on your own because every motherfucker will try to take advantage of you."

Samuel remarked, "We will do anything to complete our time and return safely to Mexico. If that is what it takes, we will join you. We just need to get all these human flies off our back."

"We are like tribes in prison and converted into animals by the authorities because they treat us that way," chuckled Enriquez. "My top camarades will have to take a vote on inducting you into La Eme or the Mano Negra (Black Hand) as some call us. I will let you know in a few days."

Two days later, the prisoners were marched out into the yard. The salt air was thick and the humidity was stronger than usual. The guards were randomly searching some of the convicts for weapons, but rarely found any despite the fact that most of them were armed with shivs. Out of the corner of his eye, Alarico saw Enriquez wave. Samuel, who was coming down with a cold, strolled slowly behind Alarico.

Enriquez, well protected as always, stood up and vigorously shook both their hands and stated, "Welcome to the Mexican Mafia! You are part of one the most powerful and feared organized crime groups. Just so you know, we exist in federal prisons, and state institutions in Arizona and California, but we also operate outside in main society. There are three components within the Mexican Mafia, the members, which only number one hundred and twenty. We keep those numbers small because it means a bigger piece of the pie for each one, if you know what I mean. The second are the camarades, which are the foot soldiers and they are the foundation of the organization. Both of you will be in this tier. The third are the sureños who are from southern California. We are divided into crews, and our people who are back on the outside collect what we call street tax from other gangs committing robberies, dealing drugs, or engaged in extortion. Whatever it is they have to pay. Understand?"

Alarico replied, "We understand and hopefully, you will keep some of these animals off our backs."

Enriquez chuckled, "We will put the word out that you are with us now and they will not dare fuck with you. You will see!"

Weeks later, tensions began to rise in San Quentin as more prisoners began to pour into the facility creating massive overcrowding. The pressure was building and it was about to erupt like a blast from a volcano. Several of the gangs began to prepare for war by making more shivs and wearing layered clothing, which would act like makeshift body armor. Alarico and Samuel could feel they were sitting on a powder keg.

One brisk morning, Enriquez called for a war council. He looked sullen and waited until everyone arrived and stood in a circle around him. Alarico could see all the other ethnic gangs congregating throughout the yard. Every one of them was making contingency plans.

Enriquez stated, "Camarades, I don't have to tell you everyone is walking on eggshells and it is just a matter of time before something sets off a war between gangs. You must quickly prepare yourself and always have a weapon with you when we are let out into the yard. We have to be together at all times. No one is allowed to go for walks alone. You will fight and protect the man closest to you. The group that really worries me is the Aryan Brotherhood. They are treacherous cabrones. Keep your ears to the ground and if you hear anything make sure you let me know immediately. Understand?"

Less than two days later, while everyone was under lockdown, a piece of paper attached to a long string and a bar of soap began to slide from cell to cell. It was called a "kite" and used by inmates to quickly send messages from cell to cell. Inmates helped push it along until it reached Enriquez. It read, "Black Guerrilla Family wants to meet with you."

The next morning, Enriquez and Leroy Jenkins, the leader of the black gang met in an isolated corner of the yard away from prying eyes. Jenkins was a monster of a man. He was extremely tall and weighed over three hundred pounds. It was rumored that he had sent a man to the promised land with one thunderous blow to the head. He was serving a life sentence for rape and armed robbery.

"What is it that you want to discuss with me?" asked Enriquez. "I hope that you are not wasting my time."

Jenkins smiled revealing several gold teeth. He replied, "Fuck no, man! I have a snitch who told me the motherfuckers from the Aryan Brotherhood are going to strike against us very soon. They want to control drug distribution in the prison and the only way they can do it is by trying to kill us. The fucking rednecks can't even spell cat and they want to move against both of our gangs."

Enriquez, rather pensive, asked, "How reliable is your snitch? I don't believe in going to war unless it is absolutely necessary."

"The snitch is one of their own," answered Jenkins. "I give him a little heroin every once in a while, and he keeps me informed on what they are planning. When the bastards make their move, all we have to do is attack them together and fuck them up. Are you with us, bro?"

"We will unite forces and all my men are already armed to the teeth," acquiesced Enriquez. "I have never liked those racist assholes. They are dumb fucking hillbillies."

One evening, Alarico and Samuel, after the lights were turned off in their cellblock, began to discuss the situation in a whispered voice. They were wary of other prisoners, or even worse, guards hearing what they were saying.

Alarico commented, "Samuel, this place is full of a bunch of crazy rats. It is an insane asylum where nothing makes sense. We will have to survive at all costs so we can get out alive. The longer we stay, the more likely we will die in this shithole."

"I agree, this place is full of drama and no one wants to live in peace," stated Samuel. "I think a gang war is going to happen any day now and we have to be prepared to slaughter people. It is a way of life here. No one is happy unless they have blood on their hands."

Prison officials soon began to question inmates in their administrative offices. They had heard rumors about an imminent gang war and wanted to avert it any way possible. They eventually brought in Alarico in shackles into one of the interview rooms. A few minutes later, a short, black man entered the room. His name was Fred Steele and he was a captain in charge of the day shift in the prison. He was a brutal man and had been reprimanded in the past for his mistreatment of the inmates. Steele was despised and feared by most of the prisoners.

Steele grinned and said, "Alarico, you are from Mexico are you not? You can help yourself by telling me about this rumor regarding conflict between the gangs."

"Yes, I am from Mexico, but I have not heard anything about what you are talking about," answered Alarico.

"You speak English pretty well," mumbled Steele. "I guess you have been studying hard. If anyone knows about this potential situation it would be you. I've seen you talking with that dirtball Enriquez."

Alarico declared, "I really have not heard anything and you are wasting your time."

Steele fumed and without warning punched Alarico in the face knocking him off his chair. Semi-conscious, Alarico felt a sharp kick to his upper back and he fainted. Two guards had to carry him back to his cell. Samuel was staring at him when he woke up.

"What the hell happened to you?" inquired Samuel. You look like a truck ran over you and then backed up and did it again."

Alarico moaned and stated, "It was that cabron guard, Steele, who hit me. He wanted me to tell him of the pending war. Apparently, he has snitches who keep him informed. He got mad because I refused to tell him anything, but he will pay for hitting me."

Three days passed and the prisoners began to pour slowly into the yard. The sky was cloudy and the wind made a whistling sound as it came over the tall prison walls. Very quickly, the hardened criminals divided themselves into their respective gangs. A few minutes went by and suddenly loud yells filled the air as thirty members of the Aryan Brotherhood charged straight at the Mexican Mafia. It was reminiscent of a medieval battle as bodies slammed against each other and shivs began to violently penetrate flesh and bone. The Black Guerilla Family joined the battle and hit the right flank of the Aryan Brotherhood. Screams of pain grew louder and louder. Alarico slashed the necks of two white supremacists and plunged his makeshift knife into the eye of a third one. Guards began firing tear gas canisters into the yard and the thick fumes billowed into the air. It caused major irritation to the prisoner's eyes, mouth, throat, and lungs, but their adrenaline was at optimum levels and they kept fighting. Gunshots came from the guard towers and everyone was ordered to get on the ground. Initially, that didn't work. To his right, Alarico saw Steele trying to skirt the melee. Alarico quickly chased him down and the last thing Steele felt was a sharp shiv plunge deep into his chest with a thud. It severed his aorta and he bled out in seconds.

More shots rang out and this time the guards fired into the inmates killing five of them instantly. The use of lethal force caused the prisoners to lay on the ground in submission.

Blood was everywhere and mangled corpses were scattered throughout the yard. One man was completely decapitated and his severed head still had a smirk on it. The Aryan Brotherhood lost fifteen men in all and the Black Guerilla Family and the Mexican Mafia each lost two of its members. Alarico and Samuel suffered minor stab wounds to the arms. An investigation was launched, but didn't amount to much since none of the inmates cooperated and most claimed self-defense.

The Mexican Mafia revered Alarico and Samuel for their savagery and bravery during the bloody gang war. They were looked up to by the inmates and left alone for the remainder of their prison sentence. Their ties to the Mexican Mafia would later prove to be advantageous to Alarico and Samuel. After what appeared like an eternity, but was only twelve months, the two friends were released and immigration officials deported them to Mexico through Tijuana.

CHAPTER 4

FROM CRIMINAL TO COP

Once in Tijuana, Alarico and Samuel made their way to a bus station and purchased one-way tickets on ACN Autobuses to Guadalajara, Jalisco. They used money the Mexican Mafia had provided them. It was not a lot, but it would support them for a couple of weeks until they hopefully found a job. Alarico had a cousin, Felipe Montes, who lived in the city and would help them. Alarico and Samuel sat on hard plastic chairs until their departure was announced on a squawky loudspeaker. They scrambled along with several other people to get on the brown/green bus. Many carried heavy suitcases and unintentionally banged them against the other passengers who immediately gave them dirty looks. The two friends were able to get seats together towards the back. The bus was dirty and appeared as though it had not been cleaned in months. There were food wrappers, half eaten tacos, potato chips, and even used condoms on the floor. The only thing missing were the rats who would have considered it heaven. After everyone had climbed aboard, the bus driver shifted gears and the long, sleek vehicle shuddered and started to move slowly out of the parking lot. Alarico and Samuel leaned back and relaxed. They were elated to be free and no longer having to live in cages like animals.

After several hours and numerous stops at more bus depots to pick up other passengers, the packed bus arrived in Guadalajara, which was Mexico's second largest city. They quickly hailed a cab that drove them to Felipe's house. It was in a poor neighborhood, but the residence was well maintained and had manicured bushes in front. After paying the cab driver, they walked to the front door and knocked loudly. Seconds later, Felipe opened the door and smiled broadly. He was a short, thin man with thick, brown hair.

Felipe commented, "Primo, it is so good to see you after so many years. I didn't expect you for a few more days. As they say in Mexico, my house is your house. Who is your friend?"

Alarico chuckled, "This is my best friend, Samuel. We grew up together. We appreciate you putting us up for a while until we can get a job and get a place of our own."

"Please, come into my humble house," responded Felipe. "I live here alone since my wife died in a car crash three years ago and my only daughter is now married and lives with her husband in Hermosillo, Sonora. I fixed up a bedroom for each of you and please help yourself to whatever is in the refrigerator. I put some Tecate beer in there for you."

Alarico replied, "I heard about your wife and was very sorry she died so tragically. It seems life brings us more pain than joy, but we have to take the good with the bad. I could sure use one of those beers right about now."

Felipe hustled into the kitchen and returned quickly with three ice cold bottles. After distributing the alcoholic beverages all of them sat on mismatched chairs in the small living room.

Felipe asked, "What kind of job are you looking for? I know a lot of people and may be able to help you. I work with the state government as an assistant to the personnel director. He is very tight with the governor."

Samuel responded, "I personally don't care what the work is as long as it doesn't involve manual labor. Those poor souls work like fucking dogs and get paid slave wages."

Taking a sip of his beer, Alarico laughed, "I have to agree with Samuel on the matter. Not only do laborers get paid shit, but also people don't respect them and treat them like garbage. What jobs are currently available?"

Felipe answered, "The Jalisco State Police is now hiring a lot of new officers. Many of the police forces across the state are trying to get more manpower because they are being outgunned by the drug cartels."

Samuel howled in laughter, "Do you think they would actually hire us? We just got out of prison! There is no police force in the world that would employ us."

"That is where you are wrong," smiled Felipe. "Most of the police in Mexico have criminal records. No one is going to know that you served time in the U.S. Do you think Americans share that information with our country?"

Alarico, tapping his forefinger on the armrest, stated, "Felipe, that is a good point you make. Besides, I hear they make a lot of money on bribes. Can you get us some applications?"

"I will get you some tomorrow when I go the office," replied Felipe. "I will also help you fill them out since I know what qualifications they are looking for. We can make it all up since they never check references, education, or work experience. It is all such a farce."

After getting drunk, all three went to bed, however, Alarico lay awake staring at the dark night through his window. He was greatly amused by the different twists and turns in life, which destiny decided for everyone in a very whimsical way. Their friends in the Mexican Mafia would be totally astonished if they knew the career path he and Samuel were contemplating. Alarico decided it was probably best they didn't know. He turned on his side and soon fell asleep.

The next day, Felipe left for work early in the morning. Alarico and Samuel sat at the kitchen table eating scrambled eggs, bacon, and warm tortillas. It was quite a change from the repetitive, bland food they had been eating in prison.

Alarico commented, "Samuel, how do you feel about

joining the state police? Personally, I look at it as a great stepping-stone to bigger and better things. It is nothing more than a beginning for us."

"You are absolutely right," agreed Samuel. "It is better than engaging in petty theft, which is not very lucrative. We need to move away from that and become much more sophisticated in what we do. Money and power are the things we need to strive for and be methodical so we don't make stupid mistakes."

"You make a lot of sense," retorted Alarico. "Going back to prison is not an option, especially one here in Mexico. They are nothing more than pigsties."

That evening, Felipe returned to the house with the applications as he had promised. He sat around the table with Alarico and Samuel and they began to fill them out with fabricated information. They didn't disclose their criminal record and falsified they had both graduated from high school in Mexico City. The only accurate thing on their applications were their names. All three of them laughed loudly at the outrageous falsehoods. Within an hour, the forms were completed and Felipe admonished Alarico and Samuel to memorize the information on the forms in the event they had to go through an interview.

Two weeks later, after Felipe had submitted the applications and pushed some buttons, Alarico and Samuel received a letter asking them to come to state police headquarters that

Friday at three in the afternoon. On the appointed day, the two friends took a cab to a large three-story building that was full of black police cars in the front parking lot. Uniformed police, like ants, came in and out of the building. Alarico and Samuel walked into a cavernous lobby and talked to one of the officers standing nearby. He directed them to an office on the third floor. The sole elevator was packed so they decided to take the stairwell. The stairs were severely chipped and a small dead rat was lying in a corner with its teeth sticking out and its tail pointing straight up in the air. They quickly found the office they were supposed to report to and entered a very small reception area where an old woman, with unruly, gray hair, sat behind a cheap desk. She was on the phone and waved for them to take a seat. A few minutes later, she signaled them to enter the doors, which had big, gold letters, "Marcos Trujillo, Jefe de Investigaciones." As they went in, a large man with an Emiliano Zapata mustache was zipping up his pants, and a beautiful policewoman was pushing her skirt down. She smiled and quickly walked out the door.

Trujillo smirked and said, "You must be the two idiots that are applying for jobs, right?"

"Yes, we are looking for work and thought being policemen would be a great profession," answered Alarico. "We want to serve our country and protect it from crime."

Trujillo responded, "Cut the bullshit. We have over five thousand sworn officers and not a single one is here to protect and serve. I have a few questions to ask you. Are you citizens of Mexico and have a high school education? Do you have criminal records or currently use illegal drugs? Oh, and before I forget, are both of you at least eighteen years old?"

"Yes, to your first question and no, to your second one," smiled Alarico. "We are both twenty years old."

Trujillo, with a serious frown on his brow, stated, "OK, the interview is complete and we will let you know within a week if you are going to be hired."

Perplexed, Alarico inquired, "I don't understand, the interview is over? I thought it would be much longer!"

"What the fuck, can't you see that I am a very busy man!" yelled Trujillo. "This is the standard interview we give to each and every applicant. Now, get the fuck out!"

Alarico and Samuel left and were greatly amused regarding the ludicrous interview, which only lasted a minute. The initial prison interview at San Quentin lasted much longer. It was insane and completely laughable.

Later that evening, Felipe asked if the interview had gone well. He was concerned that everything had gone smoothly and Alarico and Samuel hadn't tripped up on the false information on their applications.

Samuel chuckled loudly, "Felipe, it was a total joke. When we entered the office of the man who interviewed us, he had just finished having sex with a female officer. Then he asked us a few questions and that was it. He told us we would be notified soon."

"Well, it really doesn't surprise me," stated Felipe. "The police in Mexico are very arrogant and corrupt. Quite frankly, it was good for both of you that he didn't ask too many questions."

Alarico chimed in, "I have never even asked you, but what is the pay for a state police officer here in Jalisco?"

"Unfortunately, the pay is actually quite dismal," replied Felipe. "It is nine thousand pesos ($900 U.S.), per month, but while you are at the training academy, it will be half of that. But not to worry since you will make at least five times your regular salary in bribes. Everyone will give you good money to look the other way, especially the drug traffickers. Every police officer in the state of Jalisco is on the take."

After eight days, Alarico and Samuel finally received a letter saying that they had been selected to attend the training academy, which would begin in a week. In order to be sworn in as a state police officer they had to successfully complete all of the training requirements.

Alarico giggled, "Samuel if the academy is like the interview, it will be a piece of cake. The letter says the training is for five months, which seems like a long time, but in reality, it really isn't. One good thing is that we are in great shape thanks to the workouts in prison."

"Who the hell would have thought we would become

policemen," shrieked Samuel. "None of our friends would ever believe it. Let's have some beers and a few shots of tequila to celebrate a new beginning."

With great anticipation the time finally arrived and Alarico and Samuel reported to the police academy located on a large hill on the western outskirts of the city. The academy consisted of several buildings with an odd two-tone color of yellow and a dull red. One of the buildings had a large sign in black and white letters, which read, "Academia de la Secretaria de Seguridad Publica," (Academy of the Secretariat of Public Security). Most of the area was covered in cracked cement and almost devoid of trees and other plant life. All sixty cadets gathered at a large gymnasium where they were issued cheap, blue uniforms with matching baseball caps.

A large, fat man, wearing a police uniform three sizes too small, walked slowly to where everyone was seated. He stood there for several minutes glaring at everyone with a threatening look.

Finally, he spoke, "My name is Lieutenant Avalos and I am the director of this academy. You have been selected to be police officers of the prestigious state police. But please remember, you will not be hired if you fail to successfully get through the academy. During the training, you will undergo physical and psychological testing every second of the day. My instructors will teach you everything you need to know, so please pay close attention to them and do your very best. Does everyone understand?"

Everyone remained silent. A few minutes later, they retired to their dormitories, which were as bare as the prison cells in San Quentin. Alarico and Samuel shared a room, which had two small beds and the floor was made of cement. The restrooms and showers were communal.

Each day, the entire class made up of men and women, mostly men, were taken for an early run around the academy compound. This was followed by an hour of self-defense tactics. The remainder of the day was dedicated to courses in criminal law, search warrants, interrogation, crime scene investigation, leadership, homicide investigations, drug investigations, and other relevant subjects.

One day, the head of the Jalisco State Police, Juan Sanchez, came to the academy to speak to the cadets. He was a tall, lanky man who walked with the aid of a wooden cane. It was rumored the husband of a woman he had been having an affair with had shot him in the leg. He stood behind a lectern, which had two microphones.

"Good morning everyone," remarked Sanchez. "I came to talk to you about what it means to be a police officer and your dedication to our great state. The highest calling anyone can have is public service and yours is one of the most important professions since it deals with maintaining civil order. It is also one of the most dangerous careers because you will deal with the most violent criminals in the world. You must ensure our institution is one of integrity and uncompromising principles. Do your very best and you will be triumphant."

Everyone clapped at his brief remarks, except Alarico and Samuel who knew it was all political bullshit. The state police was one of the most corrupt agencies in the country.

After several weeks, the training became monotonous and totally repetitive. Alarico and Samuel breezed through both the physical and classroom work. It was all too easy. Anyone with the brain of a canary could pass the academy. Besides the training was poor at best. Most of the cadets thought the instructors came from insane asylums on work release programs.

One morning, a female cadet by the name of Claudia was found stabbed to death behind one of the buildings. She was lying in a pool of blood and her eyes were wide open looking up at the sky as though searching for an angel to guide her to heaven. She was one of the smartest cadets and was gifted with incredible beauty. It sent shockwaves through the cadet corps.

Fortunately, it was solved a few days later when tapes from a nearby security camera were reviewed by academy staff. Another cadet, Rogelio Santana, from Zapopan, Jalisco was arrested for the brutal murder. Apparently, he had started a love affair with Claudia and when she tried to break off the relationship, he flew into an uncontrollable rage and killed her by stabbing her over thirty times. He was later convicted and sent to prison for forty years.

With great anticipation, graduation finally came and not soon enough for Alarico and Samuel who wanted to do something more exciting. In a morning ceremony, the cadets were given their diplomas, which had more gold seals than the Magna Carta. The day before they had been given their assignments and most of the cadets, including Alarico and Samuel, would be working at central police command in Guadalajara.

When they reported to duty, they were given new tactical style uniforms, which were solid black. They were also assigned a fairly new black, Dodge Ram 2500 heavy-duty truck. It had large gold letters on each side, which read, "Policia Estatal." Alarico and Samuel felt like kids who had been given new toys to play with.

The weeks passed slowly. Alarico and Samuel continued to patrol the busy streets of Guadalajara. Each day, they would stop at different taquerias and because of their uniform were given as many savory tacos as they could eat without paying anything.

It was a bright, sunny day when they received a radio transmission advising there was a barricaded suspect at 1045 Calle Malpica who had already killed his wife and was holding his father-in-law hostage. They quickly put on their siren and emergency lights and dodged cars until they arrived at the small, brown stucco-covered house with a five-foot chain-link fence around it. Two other police officers were already on the scene and gunfire was being exchanged.

Before Alarico and Samuel were able to get out of their truck a bullet smashed through the windshield between both of them. A few more inches to the left and it would have hit Alarico in the head. They quickly jumped out and ran to join the other two officers who were hiding behind their police vehicle. One of the officers advised the suspect had killed his wife because she was going to divorce him and now was threatening to kill her father. Just then, more shots rang out and bullets bounced off the pavement close to them.

A male voice yelled out from the house, "You better leave! This is a family matter and if you don't go, I will kill my father-in-law. Do you hear me?"

He fired more rounds hitting the police cars and yelled a barrage of profanities out the window. Alarico had Samuel and the other two officers cover him. The police officers began to fire at the front of the house. The crash of broken glass could be heard as projectiles shattered the windows. Alarico sprinted rapidly around the house and was able to open a window near the back door. He crawled through it and cautiously made his way through the house. He peered through an open door in the kitchen and was able to get a clear view into the living room. There was a petite woman in a white dress literally covered in blood lying motionless near a pink sofa. An elderly man with white hair lay next to her. His arms and legs were bound with rope, but he was still alive. Looking out the front window was a tall, well-built man brandishing a 9mm handgun. He had several boxes of ammunition on a chair next to him.

Seconds later, he, once again, began to fire at the police officers outside and howl like a crazed person. Within minutes, he ran out of bullets and began to load his gun. In a flash, Alarico charged into the room and pointed his gun at the man who looked up and smiled. He dropped his weapon, put his hands in the air, and surrendered. Alarico walked up to him silently and returned the smile while squeezing the trigger. A loud blast reverberated throughout the room and the shooter stood there for a second until blood poured from his forehead. His eyes rolled back into his sockets and he fell back against the wall.

A week later, Alarico, Samuel, and the other two officers were given medals of honor by the Governor of Jalisco, Victor Quintero, a powerful politician from the dominant Mexican political party known as the PRI (Partido Revolucionario Institucional). The governor was a handsome man with bluish eyes and black hair. He had an affinity for black suits and flashy ties. It was well known in the state that he had dozens of mistresses at his beck and call.

Standing behind a podium adorned with the seal of Jalisco, Quintero addressed over three hundred police officers, "I am honored to present these well-deserved medals to four brave officers who put their lives on the line to rescue a hostage from a crazed man who had already violently killed his wife of many years. Police work is a very dangerous profession, but one filled with tremendous acts of courage and sacrifice. Please accept my eternal gratitude for preserving the peace in our great state."

Amid cheering and loud whistling, the governor placed large, silver medals with red, white, and green ribbons on the necks of the officers and vigorously shook their hands. Alarico and Samuel could have cared less about the medals and gave each other a smug look.

One particular day, Alarico and Samuel were more than famished and decided to go to Taqueria Paraiso and get some tacos. The restaurant was nothing more than a hole in the wall. It only had five tall tables and rusty, metal stools. Towards the back was a large grill, which sprayed grease on the walls and floor. They each ordered half a dozen steak and cheese tacos and filled them with pico de gallo salsa. No one dared asked them for money and the owner just smiled as they left. Waiting outside was a local prostitute sporting a huge black eye and abrasions on her arms.

Alarico asked her, "Who did this to you? You should go see a doctor and make sure you are alright."

The prostitute replied, "It was my boyfriend who hit me after snorting cocaine all day. He flew into a rage for no reason and began to beat me. I was lucky to escape and I will not be going back to him. He is a drug dealer and I hope you can put him in jail where he belongs."

Samuel probed, "Can you give us this bastard's address? And what is his name?"

With a pained look on her face, she stated, "Of course, he lives about twenty minutes from here at 14632 Calle Gaspar. It is a green-colored house with a white porch. You can't miss it. His name is Roberto Macias."

Traffic was light and they soon arrived at the house and parked a block away. Walking through a trash littered back alley, the two friends quickly approached the back door. Samuel reared back and kicked it open with a loud bang. As they rushed into the house, they immediately saw two men sitting on a brown sofa sniffing lines of cocaine from a glass coffee table. They were startled and scared by the loud forced entry.

Alarico and Samuel pointed their weapons at their heads and told them to get on the floor. They obeyed and laid flat on their stomachs.

Alarico asked, "What are your fucking names? We got reports from neighbors saying you were playing loud music and disturbing the peace."

The man with a beard looked up and stated, "My name is Roberto and he is my cousin, Santiago."

While Samuel held them at gunpoint, Alarico searched

the house and in one of the bedrooms found about two hundred thousand dollars in pesos. Hidden under a pile of dirty clothes, he also discovered four kilos of cocaine wrapped tightly in green plastic. He put the money and cocaine into an athletic bag, which he removed from the closet. With a wide grin on his face, Alarico walked back to where Samuel was guarding the two men. He glanced at Samuel who looked at him with a puzzled look. Alarico took out his handgun and shot each man in the head twice. They didn't see it coming.

Samuel yelled, "What the fuck did you do that for? They were not putting up any resistance."

Alarico opened the bag and showed him the money and cocaine. Samuel chuckled and he slapped Alarico on the back and both hugged each other. Silently, they made their way back to their police vehicle and left.

Late one night, Television Azteca reported one of the governor's bodyguards from the state police had been killed in a botched robbery attempt. Two teenagers, both seventeen years of age, were arrested for the crime. They had tried to take the officer's wallet, not knowing who he was, and when he resisted, they shot him four times.

Forty-eight hours later, Alarico was notified he would take the dead bodyguard's place. The governor had specifically asked for him. Alarico was taken aback, but looked at it as a great opportunity. He promised to try to get Samuel into the prestigious protective detail.

Three days later, Alarico traveled to the Governor's Palace. It was an imposing baroque two-story building beset with snarling gargoyles. It was here that Father Miguel Hidalgo y Costilla, a Mexican Roman Catholic priest, issued his famous proclamation demanding the abolishment of slavery and the end of Spanish rule on September 16, 1810. Alarico ran up the stairs and was quickly confronted by a guard, but allowed to enter once he identified himself. He went directly to the governor's office on the second floor. A beautiful, young receptionist told him to go right in since the governor was expecting him. Alarico entered with his head held high. Governor Quintero stood up and went around his desk to shake his hand.

Quintero stated, "Alarico, welcome to the palace. The first time we met, I knew you were special and wanted to get you on my protective detail. It will not be an easy job since my hours are long and erratic, but I know you are up to the task."

"Thank you, governor, it is an honor to be able to work for you," answered Alarico. "I have a favor to ask. I have worked very closely with Samuel, another officer you gave a medal to, and would like to get him on the detail with me. He is a fearless officer and extremely intelligent."

Laughing, Quintero replied, "You have been in my office for less than five minutes and you are already asking me for favors. Not a problem, I will give the order to have him reassigned here. I just wanted to welcome you onboard. And by the way, get rid of your police uniform. While working as my bodyguard, you will wear a suit."

"Thank you, governor," commented Alarico. "You will not regret your decision. We will be the best bodyguards you ever had."

Excited, Alarico called Samuel and gave him the good news. Samuel was equally thrilled. He was happy to be with his friend. They had become inseparable. In less than twenty-four hours, Samuel received his transfer orders reassigning him to the governor's office.

The skies were dark and it was beginning to rain as Alarico and Samuel made their way to work. As soon as they arrived the governor's secretary told them that Quintero was looking for them. Their immediate thoughts were that something was amiss. They cautiously entered his office.

Quintero in a low voice told them, "Listen, I want you to go meet a friend of mine at the El Italiano Restaurant, which is located at Golfo de Cortes No. 4134. He has something for me, and I need you to go pick it up. I would go myself, but I have a meeting with a couple of mayors. My friend's name is Arturo. He will be wearing a black suit and a white shirt."

The two friends borrowed one of the governor's unmarked cars. It took them half an hour to get to the restaurant. They were impressed with the interior, which had immaculate white walls and a wooden ceiling. The tables were covered in white linen tablecloths. They were adorned with matching napkins and shiny, crystal water goblets. It was spectacular. Sitting at the back wall, they saw the person described by the governor. They immediately recognized him as Arturo Cardenas, the sinister leader of the Azteca Cartel. It was the most violent and feared drug trafficking organization in Mexico. The cartel had drug distribution tentacles in over fifty countries, including the United States. Their annual revenue was estimated at more than forty billion dollars.

Cardenas was tall, of medium build, and had unusual catlike green eyes. He wore huge diamond rings on both hands. His thick black hair was long and combed to the back. He looked more like a movie star rather than a drug capo. The feared cartel leader had at least thirty bodyguards sitting at tables around him. As Alarico and Samuel approached where Cardenas was sitting, they noticed a large, black Samsonite suitcase next to his right leg.

Cardenas stood up slowly and remarked, "The governor must have sent you. Come sit down. We just ordered a lot of food and a few bottles of tequila. I am sure we will be seeing each other quite often and it is important to know one another."

Waiters began bringing out platters of different types of pasta, salads, and fried calamari. Everyone was served more food than they could possibly eat. A young male waiter wearing a black shirt and pants began pouring tequila into dozens of shot glasses. The amber colored liquid looked more than inviting.

Cardenas lifted his glass and toasted, "To money and power! We lifted ourselves out of poverty and never will we go down that hole ever again. We control Mexico and pull the strings of every official in the country. It is easy for us to kill those who oppose us, but sometimes it is preferable to bribe them. Salud!"

Everyone, including Alarico and Samuel downed the bitter tasting tequila and then quickly bit into a slice of fresh lime. Several more rounds followed until everyone was a bit tipsy, even the bodyguards. Very quickly, it became obvious there was a strong chemistry between the drug lord, Alarico, and Samuel.

Cardenas declared loudly, "You know, I like you guys. I like people who don't put up pretenses or act high and mighty like they are something special. I can tell you came from a poor barrio just like I did many years ago. How would you like to make some good money?"

Alarico inquired, "We are always wanting to make more money than we get as policemen. What did you have in mind?"

An evil grin came to the face of Cardenas, "There is a fucking journalist here in Guadalajara who is a thorn on my side. He is always writing stupid articles about my cartel and me. The other day, he posted my photo on the front page of the newspaper and that I don't forgive. His name is Jesus Castro. I will pay you half a million pesos ($50,000 dollars) to get rid of him. Normally, I would have one of my men do it, but it can't be tied to me. Understand!"

Alarico quickly replied, "We will do it. We need a photograph and his address, if you have it. Also, the money must be paid to us up front."

Cardenas roared in laughter, "That is why I like you. You are not stupid. Certainly, I will pay you the money tomorrow."

The drinking continued for hours with animated banter back and forth. Jokes were traded followed by prolonged loud laughter, which shook the rafters. Everyone was having the time of their lives and the booze continued to flow like the waters from the Rio Grande. At about midnight, everyone decided it was time to go home.

"Before I forget, this suitcase is for the governor," smirked Cardenas. "Please be careful with it since it is a nice little present for him. Give me your telephone number and one of my men will contact you tomorrow. He will give you the money and information on the fucking reporter."

Swaying back and forth from the copious amounts of tequila, Alarico wrote his cell number on a piece of paper and handed it to Cardenas who in turn gave it to one of his men. Seconds later, everyone literally staggered out from the restaurant. Samuel was a little bit more sober so he took the wheel. They drove to the Governor's Palace where Quintero was sitting at his desk working on a water drainage project for the city. He laughed when he saw how inebriated they were.

Quintero remarked, "Well it looks like you two quickly made friends with Cardenas. I was beginning to wonder if you had made off with my gift, but I knew you were too smart to do that. Put the suitcase on the sofa and go home and get some rest."

On the drive home, Samuel ran a red light and was almost broadsided by a large bus, which fortunately swerved to the right. Alarico had him pull over and he drove the rest of the way home. They were so tired and drunk they went to bed with their clothes on.

Early the next day, their sleep was abruptly interrupted by a pack of wild dogs fighting each other in their backyard. Alarico jumped out of bed and grabbed his pistol. He opened the back door and fired several shots in the air causing the mangy dogs to run off in different directions. Still suffering from a throbbing hangover, Alarico and Samuel showered and headed to work. On the way, they received a call from one of Cardenas's men. He made arrangements to meet them at the cathedral located on Avenida Fray Antonio Alcalde. The man in a hoarse voice said he was already waiting for them in a red Lexus sedan. Within minutes, Alarico and Samuel saw the magnificent cathedral made of blocks of polished stone and its golden neo-gothic spires. They quickly located the Lexus and parked alongside. A thin man, exited the stylish car and opened the trunk. He was wearing a black cowboy hat and boots made with the skin of a diamondback rattlesnake. He handed them a briefcase full of money and a small photograph of Castro, the reporter, who worked for the prominent newspaper El Informador. On the back of the photo was the address of where Castro lived.

After work, Alarico and Samuel located Castro's residence. They had to drive around the area several times since most of the houses were not numbered. Samuel had to get out on foot and was finally able to identify the house. The sun was beginning to drop on the horizon. They parked across the street. Luck was on their side. In less than half an hour they saw a blue Toyota truck pull into the small driveway. It was Castro, and he entered the house in a hurry. In minutes, Castro came out in a rush and got into his truck. He pulled onto the street and headed north. The two assassins followed at a discrete distance until Castro pulled into the large parking lot of the Sagrantino Restaurant. The time and location were ripe for murder. Alarico jumped out and began walking slowly to intercept the reporter. As Castro walked to the door of the restaurant, Alarico raised his Browning 9mm and fired. The first shot hit Castro in the groin immediately turning him into a eunuch. Screaming, he fell to his knees and a second later he heard a second blast. A bullet punched a hole in his head with the force of a sledgehammer. He fell backward onto the asphalt as bodily fluids flowed freely from his corpse.

Michael S. Vigil

Castro became the fortieth reporter killed in Mexico and the year was not yet over. The profession was one of the most dangerous in the country as they had become fair game for the cartels, which were becoming less tolerant of the press.

CHAPTER 5

INTO THE WORLD OF THE CARTEL

Alarico and Samuel were constantly crossing the line between justice and criminality and they had become extremely tangled. They could no longer distinguish between right and wrong. The only thing they understood was that crime was extremely lucrative. With each passing day, both were entering more and more into a darker world where only evil prevailed. The corruption completely blinded them and money became a total obsession. Working for the governor was paying many dividends. Through sheer exposure they were meeting other governors, mayors, police chiefs, and military officers who would be of great value to them later on.

One evening, as storm clouds were beginning to gather over the expansive city of Guadalajara, Alarico and Samuel accompanied Governor Quintero to a dinner meeting with General Alfonso Beltran. The army commander was in charge of Military Zone V, which included the states of Jalisco, Aguascalientes, Colima, Nayarit, and Zacatecas.

Moving at a fast clip, they quickly arrived at the Hueso Restaurant. The outside of the establishment was painted white and was covered by black horizontal and vertical lines on its walls. The interior was white washed and had animal bones on the walls as decorations. Long, brown wooden tables provided a communal ambiance. General Beltran was seated away from the crowd towards the back and was guarded by an escort of six young soldiers. His uniform was covered in medals and ribbons. He was very tall, slender, and had a permanent scowl on his face. The governor shook hands with the general and then introduced Alarico and Samuel. The general looked at them suspiciously at first, but soon began to relax.

Not long after, waiters brought several plump, roasted chickens and Serrano peppers along with avocado filled salads. While enjoying their meal, the conversation rapidly turned to the current security issues afflicting Jalisco.

General Beltran advised, "Crime in the state has started to escalate, especially murders. Two days ago, we discovered a mass grave of thirty people, both men and women, who were tortured and dismembered. We still don't know who is responsible, but I suspect it's the Azteca Cartel. Mexico has become a giant cemetery and we have become a very cruel and vicious society. Life has no meaning anymore."

"But there is no evidence it was the Azteca Cartel," stated

Quintero. "We have to be careful about attaching blame on these matters, otherwise it could backfire on us politically."

The general continued, "Last night some of my soldiers who were on patrol came under attack in Tlaquepaque. Two of our trucks were destroyed by machine gun fire. Fortunately, no one was injured. The criminals now have better weapons than we do. It is truly a sad state of affairs."

Alarico piped in, "Have you ever thought of creating a joint military/law enforcement intelligence center here in Guadalajara to collect and share information? This would allow Jalisco's security forces to conduct intelligence driven operations, which would maximize your resources."

The general responded, "That is a brilliant idea. I will coordinate with the governor on this project."

After concluding the meeting, Alarico, Samuel and the governor left the restaurant. They had eaten so much and the hot peppers had given them severe heartburn.

Sitting in the back seat, the governor spoke up, "Alarico, are you fucking crazy? We want to do less, not more on counterdrug efforts. If we start to go after the drug traffickers, they will come after us with a vengeance, which also means no more bribes."

Alarico answered, "It will be a big political coup for you. Have a press conference and tell them of your plan. You limit the information to nothing more than unusable bullshit. This will permit you to cover your tracks since the press is always making allegations the Azteca Cartel has you in their pocket. Does that make sense?"

"Fuck, I never thought of it that way," said the governor with a chuckle. "Alarico, I have to say, you are a criminal genius. You are like a master chess player in the way you think."

The governor's press secretary, four days later, called for a large press conference with General Beltran and Governor Quintero. All the television and newspaper reporters showed up with their notepads and cameras. The governor wore a black suit and a conservative blue tie. The general was in a freshly pressed uniform with gold epaulets.

The governor addressed the throng of journalists, "Thank you all for coming today. I also thank General Beltran for being here. I want to announce the creation of a joint military and law enforcement intelligence center to combat organized crime in the state of Jalisco. The center will be located in Guadalajara and we hail it as an important step to bringing peace and tranquility to our great and beautiful state."

General Beltran then stepped up to the podium and commented, "By working together and sharing relevant information, we will be able to have a greater impact on those who commit crimes in our state. Our joint efforts will provide a unified front that Jalisco has needed for quite some time."

A female reporter with disheveled black hair inquired,

"Do you believe this will allow you to dismantle the Azteca Cartel and also arrest its leader, Arturo Cardenas?"

The governor quickly responded, "I believe it will impact on all organized crime and that is our main objective. Thank you all for coming."

Eventually the intelligence center was established, which would have been a great tool, but corruption being what it was, rendered it into nothing more than a façade.

It was a dark, rainy night and Alarico and Samuel were on their way home when suddenly Alarico's cell phone rang. A deep voice on the other end said Cardenas wanted to see them immediately and was waiting for them at the Quinta Real Hotel, room 213. They made a quick U-turn and accelerated passing trucks and cars on the congested road and soon arrived at the three-story hotel, which had a concentration of manicured trees and shrubs in front. Entering the spacious lobby, they were impressed with the numerous crystal chandeliers hanging from the ceiling and oil paintings of cathedrals on the walls. Taking the stairs, the two men quickly found the room and tapped lightly on the door. A man opened it slightly and peered out suspiciously. Seeing it was Alarico and Samuel, the door opened wide and the man motioned for them to enter. There were six menacing looking men standing around Cardenas who was sitting on a green leather couch. He had a sullen look on his face.

Cardenas, scratching his chin, stated, "Thank you for

coming so promptly. I have another job for you. The mayor of Coyula, Manuel Lopez, has fallen in with my rivals from the Cartel del Diablo. He has been protecting and helping them move into my territory. Can you believe that? Into my fucking area! I want you to get rid of him. I don't want you to just kill him, but do it in a way that sends a message to others who may be thinking of betraying me. Understand?"

"We totally understand," replied Alarico. "He is as good as dead. I guess politicians think they can do things and get away without any consequences. It is so easy to get to them. Killing the hijos de puta is as easy as stepping on an ant."

Cardenas laughed loudly, "You are right, they are stupid and are blinded by money. Here is your normal payment and a photo of the fucking bastard. If you do this quickly there will be a bonus in it for you. I like the way you kill people. You are very efficient in the art of murder."

Samuel took the leather briefcase full of money and the small wrinkled photo. Within minutes, they left and headed home. Before going to bed both had three shots of tequila. The next morning, they called in sick and prepared to travel to Coyula, which was a short distance from Guadalajara. Alarico and Samuel checked and rechecked their fully automatic Ak-47s and their Colt 45s and made sure to take enough ammunition to start a small war. It was always better to take more than not enough.

The two assassins drove to Coyula located in the

municipality of Tonalá, which had a population of about thirty thousand inhabitants. Entering the small town, they passed by Barranca Lake whose water has a strange green color to it. Several aluminum beer cans bobbed up and down as the water shifted slightly. Rows of white buildings with windows framed in orange, pink, and red colors lined the area. The town was quiet and wild dogs ran through the streets unchallenged. They finally found the mayor's office located in a small building that was in need of a paint job. There were only five cars parked in front. Obviously, not a busy day for the mayor.

Alarico and Samuel parked on a quiet street nearby where they could see everyone coming in and out of the building. An hour passed by then another. Time began to move very slowly. It was also getting uncomfortable sitting in the car. Their legs and back were getting stiff and painful.

Suddenly, they saw three men come out. One of them was definitely Mayor Lopez. He was a short man who walked with a noticeable limp and wore a white guayabera shirt and black slacks. The other two dark-skinned men, obviously his bodyguards, were dressed less casually. Both wore blue jeans and western shirts. They entered a late model black Mercury Marquis and slowly began driving north. Several miles out they turned onto a narrow two-lane dirt road. Samuel, who was driving, overtook the car and came up alongside. Alarico put the barrel of his AK-47 out the window and riddled the car with bullets. It went off the road into a steep ditch and stopped with its engine buried in three feet of mud. Taking his time, Alarico approached the vehicle and fired two long bursts into the three motionless bodies. All were dead, including the mayor. Quickly, they yanked the mayor's body from the car. Samuel then retrieved a small chain saw from the trunk of their car and went to work. In a few minutes, he completely dismembered the body with the skill of a seasoned butcher. First the legs and then the arms. He and Alarico tied the appendages separately with rope and threw them in the trunk of their car that they had lined with plastic. They headed back to the town.

Alarico and Samuel parked near a tall pine tree on the town square. Now it was a matter of waiting until darkness set in and everything was quiet. Working as a team, they threw the ropes over a long horizontal branch on the tree and tied them so the arms, legs, and the bloody torso with the head still attached dangled in the air like macabre ornaments. Blood dripped onto a patch of white hibiscus flowers turning them totally red. Alarico and Samuel then drove away into the dark night.

The next day, the brutal killing was reported in all the media networks throughout Mexico. There was a huge public outcry, but it only lasted two days. So many other gruesome murders were occurring daily throughout the country, which diverted the public's attention from the Lopez murder. Mexico had become a massive slaughterhouse.

Alarico and Samuel, apart from working for the state police and guarding the governor of the state, had become the favorite assassins of Cardenas, the feared cartel leader. They were making decent money, but they were having to work long hours in order to comply with their government duties and the demands from the Azteca Cartel.

Cloudy skies loomed over the city of Guadalajara and threatened to unleash a torrential downpour. Alarico and Samuel had just left the governor at home and were headed to a big birthday bash for Cardenas at a ranch on the western outskirts of the city. After forty minutes, they arrived and noticed at least a hundred luxury cars and trucks parked around the opulent white mansion with red Spanish tiles on the roof. The outside was decorated with hundreds of multi-colored Chinese paper lanterns. Loud mariachi music blasted from huge amplifiers that was ear splitting. Beautiful women in tight short skirts kept pouring into the house. Heavily armed men surrounded the residence and carefully scrutinized everyone who arrived. Alarico and Samuel almost tripped over each other as they saw the recently crowned beauty queen for the state of Jalisco. She had blonde hair and stunning blue eyes. Her fitted dress showcased all of her physical attributes and matching six-inch spiked heels further elongated her curvaceous legs. The two men tried to regain their composure as their hearts almost exploded out of their chests. A waiter with a large tray of margaritas approached and offered them a glass. They each grabbed one and gulped it down. The crowd was boisterous and it was difficult to move around since the house was packed. A man tapped Alarico on the shoulder and told him that Cardenas wanted to see him and Samuel in his study. They followed the tough looking man towards the rear of the house where Cardenas sat behind a desk smoking a long Cuban cigar. He pushed himself off the chair and shook their hands.

Alarico said sarcastically, "Let me take a wild guess, you want someone eliminated from the planet, right?"

"You are too smart for your own good," laughed Cardenas. "I have a much more dangerous assignment for you and Samuel. I have been slowly expanding my territory into Mexico City, but have run into problems with Jaime Paz, the chief of police for the city. I believe he is working with another cartel. Every fucking official in the country is aligned with one cartel or the other, which means they have to be killed. They are nothing more than human chess pieces that I have to knock off the board. You know what I mean. I should mention that Paz lives in the upscale area of Bosques de las Lomas. He goes to his office in the downtown area on Paseo de la Reforma early in the morning and never deviates his route. Paz always has two armored vehicles full of armed bodyguards. Take as many of my men as you need, but get the job done. I will square it with the governor. You need to leave as soon as possible. But for now, enjoy the party and the women."

The next morning, Alarico selected twenty of Cardenas men who would form the assassination team. They armed themselves with military grade weapons and prepared to drive to Mexico City using six Dodge trucks. The trip would take slightly over six hours. Alarico and Samuel would take a commercial flight and begin to scope out the area. Later, they would all rendezvous at the Hotel Sofitel and make final plans for the attack.

That evening, Alarico and Samuel drove to the Miguel Hidalgo y Costilla International Airport in Guadalajara and boarded an Aero Mexico Airlines flight to the capital city. The trip was slightly over an hour. The plane landed at the Benito Juarez Airport and it took over forty minutes to reach the gate. The air traffic controllers were having a difficult time getting planes off the runway. Once in the terminal, Alarico and Samuel went to the Tipoa Rental Car and quickly filled out the paperwork for a Nissan Sentra. Using their cell phone GPS application, they made their way through the crippling traffic to the Secretariat of Public Security building, better known as the Mexico City Police Department. It was located at Venustiano Carranza, one of the city's sixteen boroughs. The department had a combined force of over a hundred thousand officers, but they were ill-trained and highly corrupt.

After an hour, they arrived and observed the tall, weathered concrete building with an odd vertical blue metal sculpture on its left side, which consisted of a series of X's. Several armed police officers with bulletproof vests guarded the front entrance. It was on a busy street, but they were able to park half a block away. Early in the evening, they observed two black Chevrolet Suburban's come out from the underground parking lot. The lead vehicle had its police emergency lights on as it proceeded southbound. Alarico and Samuel followed close behind. They quickly noticed the two vehicles seemed sluggish, which meant they were heavily armored. The unmarked police vehicles proceeded along Paseo de la Reforma to an opulent house in the exclusive Bosques de las Lomas area. Six uniformed men guarded the house.

Alarico and Samuel broke off their surveillance of Paz at this time and went to the Sofitel Hotel to wait for the Azteca Cartel sicarios. The twenty men finally arrived several hours later and after registering at the hotel in small inconspicuous groups, Alarico passed the word for them to meet him in an hour at a large construction site a few miles away.

The assassination team all met in a dusty field where a high-rise apartment building was being built. The workers had all gone home, which prevented prying eyes. The wind was blowing with intensity forcing Alarico to yell so everyone could hear him.

Alarico declared, "You all know what we came here for, so let's make sure we do it right. We cannot afford any mistakes and therefore we have to work closely as a team. Paz is heavily guarded and travels in an armored car. There is a second identical one with more security, which escorts him. By the way, what type of weapons did you bring and where do you have them?"

A skinny man with missing teeth responded, "We brought AK-47s, an RPG, and two .50 caliber machine guns with armor piercing ammunition. When we get ready to do the operation, the heavy machine guns can be mounted on our trucks very quickly. I also brought five hand grenades. We have them in a black panel truck with tinted windows back at the hotel. I have someone who will stay with the truck to make sure nothing happens to them until we make our move."

"That is very good news," responded Alarico. "Samuel and I will do some more surveillance of Paz and then make our final plans to kill him. Meantime, you will all keep a low profile and make sure you stay out of trouble."

Alarico saw a pile of construction helmets and orange vests nearby and told his men to take them since they might prove to be useful. Several men grabbed armloads and threw them into the bed of one of the trucks and covered them with a heavy-duty tarp.

Before dawn the following day, Alarico and Samuel, from the top of a small hill, watched Paz's house while they ate egg and red chili burritos. Dogs could be heard howling in the distance and a slight breeze rolled over the area. As the sun began to rise to the east, they saw the two black Chevrolet Suburban's return and pull up in front of the house. A minute later, Paz came out of his house wearing a dark suit and quickly entered the back seat of the second vehicle. Alarico and Samuel followed them as they turned left onto Paseo de la Reforma.

Alarico chuckled, "For being the police chief, Paz is a very stupid man. You would think that he would deviate his route to and from his house. He doesn't realize he makes himself a very easy target. I think we can make our move tomorrow."

"I agree, why waste any more time on this bastard," replied Samuel. "Once we get back to the hotel we can get together with the others and prepare the operation."

A meeting was held in Alarico's room and he laid out the assassination plan in detail. Everyone listened intently and understood what they needed to do. No one asked any questions. They went back to their rooms and would stay there until very early the next day.

The following day, the assassins began leaving the hotel at five in the morning in small groups. Some drove to the area near Chapultepec Castle and parked on the shoulder of Paseo de la Reforma. Two trucks with mounted 50 caliber machine guns waited near where Paz lived. The machine guns were mounted and expertly covered with tarps. Alarico and Samuel were also there. Before leaving the hotel, Alarico had given each team small radios he had brought with him. Communications were critical in any high-profile assassination. The trap was set and the assassins were waiting patiently for the unsuspecting prey.

At daybreak, the two Chevrolet Suburban's arrived like clockwork and picked up the police chief. As usual, they began traveling on Paseo de la Reforma and proceeded slowly because traffic was beginning to get thick. Alarico and Samuel followed the two trucks with the machine guns. As Paz and his bodyguards approached Chapultepec Castle, they noticed several men wearing hard hats and orange vests. They assumed it was a road crew. As they got closer, an RPG slammed into the front tires of the lead suburban, which careened and crashed into another vehicle. Automatic weapons fire exploded and all hell broke loose. The two trucks with machine guns came up quickly from behind and began to spray the police vehicles with thunderous fire. The armor piercing projectiles went through the vehicles like a hot knife through butter, and chopped up the bodies inside. A bullet hit the back of Paz's neck and decapitated him. His head bounced against the dashboard and then flew into the back seat. Two of the men in orange vests walked up and tossed a grenade into each of the shattered vehicles. The blasts injured several innocent pedestrians who were standing nearby. A municipal police car approached the scene with a blaring siren, but ran into a tsunami of bullets. The siren quickly went into a low moaning sound. Paz and all his bodyguards were dead. Two municipal officers and four bystanders were also slaughtered. Alarico, Samuel and the other assassins scattered in different directions and rapidly fled the city. The media, like locusts, came to the crime scene and took grisly photos of the blood and gore. Those photos were plastered on the front page of every newspaper in Mexico the following day. The president of Mexico made a brief statement condemning the act, but assured the public that his "abrazos y no balazos" (hugs and not gunshots) policy was working in reducing much of the violence.

Three days passed and Alarico and Samuel went to meet with Cardenas at Bruno's Restaurant, a five-star establishment, in Guadalajara. They ordered pit barbequed goat, corn tortillas, and several bottles of expensive tequila.

Cardenas lifted his shot glass and toasted, "To a job well done, my friends. I have an offer to make. Come work for me full-time and I will pay ten times what you are now making. Most of the people that work for me are stupid. I need smart men such as you. Deal?"

Alarico looked at Samuel and then responded, "Well, we

have been doing more work for you anyway and what you offer in terms of money is a great motivator. We accept!"

Cardenas was elated and shouted, "Welcome to the Azteca Cartel. Now you will become feared and powerful. There is nothing better in this world."

CHAPTER 6

DRUGS, DRUGS, AND MORE DRUGS

After taking the total plunge into the Azteca Cartel, Alarico and Samuel began to quickly orient themselves on the extensive operation of the transnational organized crime network. Knowledge was power. Less than a month after joining the Azteca Cartel, Cardenas had a meeting with Alarico and Samuel.

Cardenas told them, "I have decided to put both of you in charge of coordinating the tons of cocaine we are getting from our associates in Colombia. I want you to travel there and meet with Alvaro Santos, the leader of the "Clan del Golfo Cartel (Gulf Clan Cartel). First, I want to give you a little bit of history. The cartel started out as a self-defense force and was initially called Los Urabeños and then Clan Usuaga. They are a vicious right wing paramilitary group and are not to be fucked with. They take no prisoners, if you know what I mean. They are one of the most powerful cartels in Colombia with over three thousand members and make their money selling tons of cocaine. For years, they have been my primary source of supply."

Alarico inquired, "What can you tell us of Santos? He must be a very interesting man to say the least. I have heard of the Colombian paramilitaries and they are supposed to be a treacherous group of people."

Cardenas laughed, "All criminals are not to be trusted. We are all like rattlesnakes just waiting for the time to strike and kill friends and enemies alike. Never forget that! Only one thing brings us together and that is money. Santos is no exception. He is a ruthless and cunning man. Years ago, he killed his boss and through sheer force and violence became the head of the cartel. Like many of us, he comes from poverty. He grew up in the slums of Manizales, which is the capital of the department of Caldas. I know at a young age he committed petty crimes such as burglaries and robberies. Santos is not a man to be trifled with, understand?"

Alarico commented, "You are right! Samuel and I should meet him if we are going to be handling the transport of cocaine from Colombia to Mexico. We will make arrangements to travel day after tomorrow. I will give you our flight information so you can call Santos and let him know we are coming."

"My friend, I can tell you have never traveled outside the country," laughed Cardenas. "Have you never heard of a passport? You also need a visa to enter most countries. Not to worry, you will take my Lear jet, which is in a private hanger at the airport. You will fly to the coastal city of Barranquilla and Santos will have his contacts at the airport facilitate your entry. When you return, I will have a contact at the Centro de Emisión de Pasaportes (Passport Issuing Centre) give you and Samuel a passport with fictitious names. I will call Santos with your itinerary."

Two days later, Alarico and Samuel drove to the Guadalajara International Airport, early in the morning, and went to the large hanger where Cardenas had his Lear jet. His two pilots were already waiting with cups of coffee in their hands. They had filed a flight plan an hour earlier. The pilots previously worked for a commercial airline, but were recruited by Cardenas to fly for him instead. He was paying them three times what they had made and they were more than eager to please. The four of them boarded the sleek, white and blue aircraft. It taxied onto the runway and minutes later was cruising at twenty-five thousand feet heading in a southerly direction. Over an hour later, Alarico looked out the window and saw the blue colored waters of the Caribbean Sea. He took a nap and woke up as the plane was making its final approach into Barranquilla. The city, a bustling seaport, was the capital of Colombia's Atlántico Department, which was flanked by the large Magdalena River.

The Lear jet bounced once on the runway and then stabilized when the breaks were gradually applied. It quickly taxied to where private aircraft were lined up in neat rows. As they exited the plane, Alarico and Samuel noticed a dark, blue Toyota 4Runner parked a few yards away. Two tall, muscular men standing in front of it stared intently at Alarico and Samuel and then waved.

The older of the two men stated, "Welcome to Barranquilla. I hope your trip was not too long. We are here to take you to meet our boss, Alvaro Santos. He is waiting to see you. Come let us go. Don't worry about immigration or customs. They have been taken care of."

They drove through the busy streets of Barranquilla. After passing the bright yellow San Antonio de Salgar Castle, they began to parallel the Magdalena River.

The older man, who was driving, declared, "The Magdalena River is the principal river in the country. It is over fifteen hundred kilometers long. It is named after Mary Magdalene and it flows northward into the Caribbean Sea. Many organizations, including ours, use it to smuggle a lot of cocaine."

After a long bumpy ride, the men arrived at a large compound with several houses and a large warehouse. Providing security were over a hundred men armed with AR-15s and AK-47s. They parked and walked to a brown house with a large porch filled with rustic wooden chairs. Entering, Alarico and Samuel noticed racks of long weapons along the wall. Sitting at a table in the dining room was Santos. He was in his late forties and had shoulder length, dark hair. His beard was long and unkept. Santos was eating a large pargo rojo (red snapper) with coconut rice and chasing it down with a large glass of rum. Santos wiped off his mouth with his shirtsleeve and stood up. He shook Alarico and Samuels hands with his greasy paw.

Santos, spitting out pieces of fish, spoke, "Welcome! Tell me, how is my good friend Cardenas? It is good we meet since we will be coordinating the smuggling of many tons of our white powder."

"Cardenas is doing well and he sends his regards," replied Alarico. "We understand the need for close coordination with you to ensure the security of the cocaine you are selling us. There are so many things, which can go wrong when moving drugs from one country to another."

Santos took a large bite of the fish and almost choked. He cleared his throat and stated, "Transporting cocaine by air has become too dangerous and it is usually only a small amount such as five hundred kilos at a time. I have come up with an idea that will increase our shipments. I want to take you somewhere and show you what I have in mind."

Santos lifted his glass and chugged the rest of the rum. Minutes later, they jumped into the blue 4Runner and four other vehicles filled with armed bodyguards following close behind. The small convoy traveled on a bumpy, makeshift road. Tall weeds thrashed against the sides of the vehicles.

After several kilometers, they came to a narrow tributary leading to the Magdalena River. The entrance was covered by thick vegetation. Alarico and Samuel were shocked to see a submarine sitting in the murky water.

Santos laughed, "This is my beautiful new toy. I hired a bunch of Russian engineers to build it at a warehouse near Bogota. I then transported it here in four sections. It took my men two weeks to put them together. The submarine is forty feet long and can carry six tons of cocaine. Four tons in the bow and two under the crew bunks. Unlike many others, this one can fully submerge for short periods of time and is powered by two tons of heavy-duty batteries.

"That is something else," marveled Alarico. "How fast and how far can it travel?"

Santos replied, "The batteries will power it for twelve hours, which is about thirty-two nautical miles. The submerged speed is about three knots. Of course, it cannot make the entire trip without assistance, which is why it has a towing ring on the nose. The submarine is designed to be towed by a larger ship until it gets close to its destination. It will then make the final leg on its own. It is slower than an airplane, but much more reliable. A plane can be detected by radar and our sub can carry much more merchandise."

Alarico asked, "Just out of curiosity, how much did it cost you to build the submarine?"

"I paid a million and a half dollars, which includes the

navigational and communications systems," answered Santos. "Even if it only makes one trip it more than pays for itself. I stand to make over two hundred million dollars on each voyage. That is a lot of money in my pocket with very little effort. By the way, Cardenas has already placed an order for five tons and it will be the maiden voyage for my submarine. He told me to coordinate the operation with you and Samuel. Come, let's go back to my place."

After returning to Santo's house, the drug lord pulled out a large, detailed map of Mexico and spread it out on the dining room table. Alarico quickly pointed to the Mexican state of Veracruz, which bordered the Gulf of Mexico. It took a few moments, but he finally found the town of Alvarado.

Alarico stated, "This is where we need you to deliver the cocaine. It is a small town consisting of twenty-two thousand people who mind their own business. The Mexican navy rarely goes to that area and they only have ten police officers we can buy off for very little money. It is close to Highway 180 and nine hundred kilometers to Jalisco. The road trip can be made in less than ten hours."

"That will not be a problem," declared Santos. "I will deliver it there in about two weeks. Before you leave, I will give you the radio frequency and call signs we will be using so you can be in contact with the submarine. Enough business, let's have a drink of good Colombian rum and toast to our future ventures."

The next morning, Alarico and Samuel were driven back to the airport and they promptly flew back to Guadalajara. They were glad to be back home and celebrated at a hole-in-the-wall taco stand. Both had carne asada tacos and then ordered a dozen more to take home with them.

The following day, a meeting was held with Cardenas and Alarico briefed him on their trip to Barranquilla. He went into detail regarding the sophisticated submarine and the pending movement of five tons of cocaine from Colombia to the area of Alvarado, Veracruz. He mentioned he would be contracting some local fishermen to offload the submarine. Once on shore the cocaine would be loaded on a tractor-trailer rig. The large bundles would be pushed to the back of the trailer and then a panel would be placed in front of the cocaine giving the illusion it was totally empty. Unless the trailer was measured from the outside no one would know that it was ten feet shorter from the inside. It was ingenious. Cardenas was impressed with the plan and gave his approval.

The very next day, Alarico dispatched the tractor-trailer rig to Veracruz. He also sent several men in four vehicles who would provide security and also help load the five tons of cocaine into the transport vehicle. They would wait in hotels in Alvarado until the arrival of the submarine.

On a hot, balmy Monday afternoon, Alarico received a cryptic telephone call from Santos saying his grandmother would be arriving in Mexico on Thursday afternoon with five shirts for him. Everything was moving as expected, but Alarico was smart enough to know in every operation there were always glitches.

By Wednesday afternoon, Alarico and Samuel arrived at Alvarado. The heat, and more so the humidity, were intense. Within an hour, they were soaked in perspiration and began to feel weak from dehydration. They stopped at a small store and bought an entire case of bottled water. They met with the men who would transport and provide security for the cocaine from the state of Veracruz to Jalisco. Next, Alarico and Samuel met with some of the local fishermen who would bring the cocaine to shore in their makeshift canoes. Everyone was ready. Alarico set up an HF/VHF/UHF radio in his hotel room and put it on a prearranged frequency. He put a do not disturb sign on the door.

Later that night, Alarico was lying on the bed thumbing through a hotel magazine when the radio began to sputter loudly. He then heard, "This is shark to albatross. Shark to albatross, over."

Alarico responded, "This is albatross, over. I copy you loud and clear. Can you hear me?"

The radio hissed, "This is shark. We will arrive in your area tomorrow evening. Based on our current speed, we estimate an arrival at eight at night. Are you ready to receive? Copy?"

"I understand and we are ready to receive," answered

Alarico. "Do not worry, everything here is ready and I will be on the radio in the event you have a delay. Over and out!"

Before going to bed, Alarico and Samuel went to a small, rustic restaurant called Mariscos Veracruz. There were only six tables and several old women dressed in long, green skirts and white blouses darted everywhere bringing food and taking orders. Alarico and Samuel ordered sopa de caguama (sea turtle soup) even though it was on the endangered species list. They also ordered a couple of Corona beers and a shot of tequila each. After leaving the restaurant, they went back to their hotel and went to sleep early. The following day would be extremely busy.

It was a hot, sticky morning when Alarico and Samuel left the hotel lugging the small HF/VHF/UHF radio with them. They went to an isolated beach area a few kilometers south of Alvarado. It was rocky and surrounded by trees. A group of fifteen fishermen in ragged clothes and wrinkled, sun-beaten skin stood smiling with their large, makeshift canoes lined up on the shore. They had navigated the waters in the Gulf of Mexico for decades and their skills and knowledge of the area were invaluable.

"Amigos, thank you for being here and helping us," stated Alarico. "If everything goes well this evening there will be much more work for you on a regular basis. Keep in mind that in our business it is important to maintain secrecy. You cannot tell anyone what you are doing. Not even your wives. Understand?"

One of the fishermen, with no teeth and rough leathery skin, responded, "We know loose lips sink ships. Our mouths are sealed because we could also end up in prison and then who would take care of our families? Our politicians only care about themselves and getting rich. There is no way we will betray you."

Alarico and Samuel passed the time playing cards and waiting for word from the submarine. The other cartel men were a few miles away with the tractor-trailer and would not come into the area until the cocaine was on shore. Alarico would call them with his cell phone and let them know when the time was right.

At about seven in the evening the radio crackled and then a transmission began to come in, "Shark to albatross. Shark to albatross. Do you copy?"

Alarico got on the radio, "Shark this is albatross. I copy. Can you hear me, over?"

The radio buzzed loudly, "We copy. Be advised we will be arriving in about two hours. We are being towed and it has been slow going. Is everything alright on your end?"

"Everything is quiet here and we are ready," stated Alarico. "We hope you don't encounter any problems, but we are standing by and unless we hear from you our men will be near the rendezvous point waiting."

An hour later, the small fleet of canoes and determined fishermen launched into the cold water. The paddled furiously against the tide and gritted their teeth.

The water splashed against the bow of the large fishing boat towing the submarine with a sturdy, yellow nylon rope. Suddenly, a powerful searchlight began to illuminate the dark night. Soon, the smugglers saw a POLA class (long range oceanic patrol ship) ARM (Mexican Navy) Reformador about half a mile away and closing fast. The fishing boat crew scurried about in a frenzy and yelled at the captain of the submarine to submerge as they severed the towline with a sharp machete. The submarine rapidly closed its two open hatches and began to sink slowly into the black waters. Twin propellers pushed it forward. Miraculously, it went underneath the naval ship, missing its hull by ten feet. It was a close call and everyone in the sub was soaked in sweat. They continued to the area where the fisherman and their canoes were waiting. The naval ship flashed its blinding spotlight on the fishing boat. Within seconds, a bullhorn blared and a voice told the crew to prepare to be boarded. Minutes later, six uniformed and well-armed marines, in a large rubber raft, approached the fishing craft and quickly swarmed onto the boat while the crew looked on with apprehension. A thorough search did not reveal any contraband. The marines quietly left and returned to their ship. The glaring light went off and the

Reformador pointed its bow northward churning the water as it gained speed.

By this time, the men in the submarine, which had surfaced, began to swiftly offload the bales of cocaine, each weighing thirty-kilograms, and pass them to the fishermen who stacked it neatly in their boats. The process moved at full tilt and within two hours the submarine was empty and the canoes were moving silently towards the shore. With military precision, the tractor-trailer was backed up as close as it could get to the beach and a line of men began loading the huge rig as soon as the canoes arrived. The men grunted as they heaved the bales to one another. In record time, the entire load was in the rig and the large panel was put securely in place concealing it.

Meantime, the fishing boat located the sub and attached another towline and began hauling it back to the northern coast of Colombia. Before it got there, the cocaine had already arrived safely in Guadalajara and was placed in a warehouse until it could be smuggled into the U.S. The fishermen were elated when they were each paid ten thousand dollars. The smuggling of tons of cocaine from Colombia into Mexico by submarine began to increase significantly. The white powder had become more prevalent in the U.S. than the clouds in the skies.

One moonlit night, Alarico and Samuel were watching CNN Español. The anchor reported opioid abuse in the U.S.

had reached epidemic proportions and tens of thousands of people were dying each year as a result. It had all started with a large pharmaceutical company called Purdue Pharma, which produced and successfully marketed oxycontin, a painkiller. The company was accused of falsely marketing the drug as being safe and not having addictive properties. It was not true! Greed in the corporate world meant more than the well-being of others.

Alarico turned to Samuel and stated, "This is a very enlightening story. It may provide us with tremendous potential to make a lot of money. I will do some research and see how we can get into that market."

Samuel chuckled, "Your brain is always working. I am surprised with all your thoughts and ideas it hasn't exploded yet. You're the ultimate illegal drug entrepreneur."

Alarico responded, "Most of the cartels in Mexico are led by men who have very little vision. It is important to have this quality. Good leaders are men and women who have imagination and are innovators. Leadership is the core of any organization and these qualities are absolutely essential. Drug cartels are only as strong as its foundation."

During the next few weeks, Alarico began to do research on the internet and quickly realized the opioid epidemic in the U.S. was caused by a combination of prescription opioids, heroin, and to a certain extent fentanyl, a synthetic opioid. He also read a research paper, which indicated that

Americans consumed eighty percent of all opioids produced in the world. Alarico soon began to narrow his focus on fentanyl. He discovered it was a potent painkiller; fifty times more powerful than heroin. He quickly found websites from numerous Chinese chemical companies, which sold fentanyl for slightly less than ten thousand dollars a kilo. They also advertised the sale of the primary precursor chemical 4-anilino-N-phenethyl-4-piperidine (ANPP) needed to manufacture fentanyl. Alarico's mind swirled with the enormous potential for trafficking tons of fentanyl to the idiot drug addicts in the U.S. The Azteca Cartel could either get the finished product from China or the precursor needed so they could make it themselves in clandestine, makeshift laboratories in Mexico. Two days later, he was able to find the process to manufacture fentanyl. It had been posted online by a Chinese chemist. Alarico was shocked with everything one could find on social media. After collecting all the information, Alarico sat down on a dreary, rainy night with Samuel.

Alarico stated, "Samuel, I have done a lot of research on fentanyl and it is truly the drug of the future. It is cheap and so easy to make. We can generate a ton of money. Think about it. Here in Mexico, many of the opium poppy fields are being fumigated with herbicides with greater frequency each year and it has become a very big gamble to traffic in heroin. With fentanyl, the risk for us will be extremely small."

"This is something we should look at trafficking, especially with the stupid Americans willing to pay good money for it," responded Samuel. "We need to jump on this very quickly so we can control the market."

The following day, Alarico and Samuel went to a safe house where Cardenas was hiding. The cartel leader was now constantly changing locations on a daily basis. He knew he was the number one target of the Mexican government. Alarico advised him of his research and the vast profits that could be made from the distribution of fentanyl. Cardenas listened intently to Alarico. Everything made sense to him. Big profits and little risk. What could be better!

Cardenas spoke up, "Alarico, this is very good news and you did your homework. Let's move forward with this. We already have well established smuggling routes and distribution chains, which can be used to get fentanyl to the U.S. consumer market, and other countries for that matter. With additional revenue, we can bribe more officials and buy more weapons. It will help us become even more powerful."

"That is fine, we will begin to make all the arrangements right away," replied Alarico. "We will keep you posted as we begin to finalize it."

In a little over a week, Alarico found the name of one of the largest chemical companies located in the Chinese capital of Beijing. It was called the Chemical and Industry Company. He called the number and a woman answered. Alarico spoke to her in English, but then quickly determined that she spoke seven languages to include Spanish. Alarico, very expeditiously, was able to order two hundred, fifty-five-gallon barrels of ANPP and also a hundred kilos of processed fentanyl. Both the precursor and the finished product would be shipped by commercial air. But before that would happen, Alarico had to wire transfer the money from Mexico to the company's account at the Bank of China. In talking to the woman, Alarico realized he could cut the cost of the fentanyl by seventy percent, if he made it himself in Mexico. Regardless, he still ordered the quantity of ready-made fentanyl to begin the initial penetration of the U.S. market.

Ten days after wire transferring the money to the Chinese company, the entire shipment arrived at the Mexico City International Airport. Both the precursor and fentanyl powder were purposely mislabeled as ingredients for the manufacture of cosmetics. Fortunately, the customs officials at the airport did not have the training to recognize them for what they were and cleared them. Members of the Azteca Cartel loaded everything in a tractor-trailer and transported them to an isolated farm house on the southern outskirts of Tepic, Nayarit. Behind the brown, flat roofed house was a barn surrounded by a barbed wire fence. Everything was offloaded and placed in a dark corner of the outbuilding.

The following day, Alarico and Samuel drove up with three other men who were in a separate black, Chevrolet Silverado truck. They rapidly took bottles of various chemicals acquired locally from the bed of the Silverado and unloaded them. These chemicals would be mixed with the ANPP, which had been delivered the day before by the tractor-trailer rig. In order to make fentanyl several ingredients were needed. The three men then unloaded several large galvanized tubs and took them into the barn. They, however, struggled unloading a heavy pill press Alarico had bought from a company in Tegucigalpa, Honduras, but finally managed to get it off the truck.

Alarico, using the recipe for fentanyl, acquired from the internet began to show the three men how to mix the chemicals in the tubs. In three hours, they had their first batch of pure fentanyl. They placed the wet mixture into large shallow cake pans and placed them under a canopy of heat lamps to dry.

Alarico addressed the three men, "As you can see it isn't a complicated process to make fentanyl. All that matters is being able to get the ANPP chemical from China and we will all be making a lot of money. From now on, you will be the ones responsible for making the drug and you will live here. For now, let's mix the hundred kilograms of the processed fentanyl with adulterants and then run it through the pill press. Each kilo with the adulterants should make about half a million pills.

With lightning speed, the Azteca Cartel began to funnel millions of fentanyl pills into the U.S. They were smuggled through the ports of entry in San Diego and Calexico, California; San Luis, Arizona; and El Paso, Texas using secret compartments in trucks and cars. Human mules also backpacked large quantities into New Mexico just east of Columbus. Each pill sold for thirty dollars apiece on the streets of America.

It was a windy night and tumbleweeds rolled aimlessly across the flat, dry desert. Coyotes roamed the terrain hunting for rabbits. Four men with large backpacks, each containing ten kilograms of fentanyl pills, crossed the border near Columbus and began walking rapidly to avoid detection. Unknowingly, they triggered an unattended ground sensor. At the Border Patrol Command Center a light blinked furiously. Immediately, five Border Patrol officers in a white and green SUV responded to the area. They figured it was the usual undocumented migrants coming across the border in search of work. The officers had all been reprimanded in the past for mistreating them. They were deplorable, redneck white supremacists who looked down on brown-skinned people. Arriving on the scene, the officers exited their vehicle and began to walk through the brush with their flashlights. Suddenly, they saw a shadow moving swiftly thirty meters in front of them.

One of the officers drew his gun and yelled, "Fucking wetbacks, we are going to kick your asses back across the border, but not before we beat you senseless."

It would be his last demeaning racist statement. Bright flashes of gunfire illuminated the darkness and the explosions disrupted the quiet night. Hours later, other Border Patrol agents drove to the area in search of their colleagues who had not responded to numerous status requests from their command center. What they found shocked them to the core. Five severed heads were grotesquely placed on the hood of the Border Patrol vehicle. Dark, sticky blood was still streaking down the front of the vehicle. A small sign next to the ghoulish heads read, "Pinches putos, learn how to respect people or the same will happen to you!" By this time, the four men with the backpacks filled with fentanyl had been picked up by other cartel members and were over a hundred miles away from the grisly scene.

CHAPTER 7

DEATH OF A CAPO

The Azteca Cartel was now making billions of dollars a year and were becoming more powerful as they were buying corrupt politicians by the bushel. Consequently, this made them the primary target of Mexico's security forces. They were conducting extra judicial wiretaps of several cartel members, family, and anyone who might make a mistake and provide a clue as to the whereabouts of Cardenas. Despite listening to hundreds of hours of conversations, they had not yielded anything of value. Cardenas had proven himself to be a very elusive cartel leader who stayed one step ahead of the law. Mexico and the U.S. were offering a combined total of ten million dollars for information leading to his capture. Cardenas was fully aware of the efforts and the reward, but he scoffed at them with complete arrogance. He was on the run and issued orders through key high-ranking cartel leaders who then relayed the orders to the rank and file. He never used phones anymore and ensured no one used them while meeting with him. Anyone within twenty kilometers from Cardenas was prohibited from using cell phones. He knew directional finding equipment could be used to pinpoint his location.

One blustery day, Cardenas was looking out the window of one of his many safe houses when he saw one of his men standing by a tree making a telephone call. Enraged, he charged out of the house with his diamond studded Colt .45 handgun and put a bullet in the back of his head. He yelled at some of his bodyguards to get some shovels and bury him in the field behind the house. Cardenas no longer had any patience and knew the slightest mistake could cost him his life or freedom. He was now constantly moving between the states of Sinaloa, Nayarit, and Jalisco. It was taking its toll on him, both physically and mentally. Paranoia was starting to set in and it was made even more acute by physical exhaustion.

A political party leader sent a message to Cardenas through a member of the cartel who delivered it person since it was death to do it by phone. It was a warning to him that a group of federal police from Mexico City had been sent to Guadalajara to track him down. Their orders were to find and kill him. He had become too powerful and could turn on the politicians if he were taken alive. Cardenas immediately felt his blood boil as it flowed through his body. It fueled his instinctive homicidal tendencies, which could only be satisfied through the spilling of blood. He quickly met with two of his most trusted and reliable assassins. One of them was a twenty-two-year-old former beauty queen by the name of Claudia. She entered the cartel when she was only eighteen through her former boyfriend who had recently died in a gun battle with a rival cartel. She could have gotten out, but opted to stay. She loved killing and was tough as nails. The other one, Jesus, was an older man who had been recruited when he left the Mexican army. He was skilled in ambushes and the use of all kinds of military weapons.

Cardenas addressed them, "I wanted to meet with you personally because I have been informed some federales have been sent to try to kill me and they are now looking for me in Guadalajara. I need for you to find and eliminate them before they get to me. It should not be a big problem locating them because they are probably staying at one of the local hotels and we have plenty of contacts in most of them."

Claudia stated, "You know their deaths are not going to stop them since the government will only send more. Are you willing to take the risk?"

"Claudia is right, they will keep sending more and more people to kill you," commented Jesus. "Sometimes it is better to try to bribe them in order to avoid riling up a political beehive."

Turning beet red, Cardenas responded, "Fuck no, I am not offering them any money. I am tired of the government pushing and pushing against me. Well, the time has come for me to push back, understand? I want you take as many men as you need to kill these putos."

Claudia and Jesus selected fifteen of the most fearless and psychopathic killers and began looking for the group of federal police. In less than forty-eight hours they hit pay dirt. One of their sources at the La Mansion del Sol Hotel confirmed twelve of them were staying there and each day would leave in the morning and not return until late at night. He was even able to give them a description of the four black Nissan SUVs they were driving.

The following day, hours before daybreak, the cartel assassins located the federal police vehicles clustered together in the hotel parking lot. They parked about a hundred yards away and waited. Claudia lit up a marijuana cigarette and took a big puff then passed it to Jesus who did the same. Soon the interior of their car was engulfed in smoke. They giggled and made silly jokes.

An hour later, the federales carrying AR-15s walked to their SUVs. Their small caravan began traveling in a southeasterly direction. The Azteca Cartel killers followed behind. A few kilometers out of the city, it became obvious they were heading to the small village of Santa Anita. Claudia decided not to follow any further and risk being compromised. She knew the federales had to come back the same way so they parked on each side of the road where they would wait. Two of them positioned themselves in a grove of orange trees where they could see two kilometers down the road. It would provide ample time for them to spring an ambush. Claudia and Jesus began smoking marijuana again and made jokes about decapitating the Mexican president and mailing his head to the U.S. president who was a good friend of his.

Claudia laughed, "With the racist immigration policy in the U.S., the head would probably be deported within hours."

"They certainly would not give it a work visa," roared Jesus. "Maybe it could get a job at the American president's golf course as an undocumented head."

They doubled up in laughter and continued smoking weed until they ran out. With a bad case of the munchies Claudia and Jesus were hoping to carry out their assignment rapidly and get back to Guadalajara to enjoy a large meal.

It was late in the afternoon and the men parked in the middle of the orange trees gave the signal the federal police were on their way back. In a mad scramble, the assassins leaped from their cars and some tripped on their AK-47s. They hid in tall grass next to the road and made sure the safeties on their weapons were off. As the vehicles began to approach, explosive bursts of gunfire swept across the road and slammed into the convoy. The police were literally cut to shreds. A couple of them managed to get out of their vehicles, but were cut in half by the barrage of lead. The assassins pulled the federales out of the cars and lined them up along the side of the road. Blood was everywhere and one of the assassins slipped on it and fell face first into the gore. Civilians who drove onto the scene were petrified they too would be killed so they honked their horns and nervously joked loudly with the murderers as if to say you did a great job and we support you.

Claudia yelled at them, "We are the Azteca Cartel and we run the state, not the federal government. We will protect you against the pinche gobierno!"

The assassins calmly walked through the bloody scene and kicked the dead bodies then decapitated them with long, sharp knives and rolled the heads down the road like they were bowling balls. Minutes later, they slowly drove away and returned to Guadalajara with a tremendous sense of satisfaction with their work. Claudia and Jesus found a seafood restaurant and ate over a kilo of lobster and drank an entire bottle of cheap vodka.

One chilly morning, Alarico and Samuel met with Cardenas in an isolated field thirty kilometers west of Guadalajara. Over thirty-five bodyguards provided security while the three cartel leaders discussed business. Cardenas had a worried look on his face and the stress of being a hunted man was beginning to show. Being constantly on the run had aged him and he now walked hunched over with his head down. His arrogance and sense of humor were gone. He was a shell of his former self.

Cardenas remarked, "My friends, I have been doing some

serious thinking this past week and have decided to take a break from this business. I am tired of moving around and being the principal target of the fucking government. I need to get some rest, a long sabbatical, if you will, in order to refresh myself. It is way too easy to make mistakes when one is tired all the time. As you know this business can easily cause your death and I am too young to die. I just feel that right now I have one foot in the grave and the other on a slippery banana peel. For this reason, I am going to leave you and Samuel as the temporary heads of the Azteca Cartel until I return. Of course, I will be in contact with you, but I cannot run the day-to-day operations always being on the run. Another thing, be careful with Claudia and Jesus. They will be jealous and could make an attempt on your lives. They are great assassins, but don't have the savvy or intellect to manage the cartel. Besides, both are addicted to marijuana and it makes them vulnerable."

Alarico replied, "Not to worry. We understand the pressures of this business. Most people think drug trafficking is easy money, but don't really understand the mental stress involved in being threatened by government forces or other traffickers who want to kill you to gain more power and wealth. It is like playing chess against multiple opponents. We can take care of ourselves against Claudia and Jesus. Where are you going?"

"I plan on hiding out in Tepic, Nayarit," replied Cardenas.

"I have a large condominium in the city. For security, I will only take twelve of my most trusted men. Well, good luck and we will be in contact soon."

Cardenas, slouched over, walked to his car and sped away followed by three other cars full of bodyguards. He felt better already. Alarico and Samuel would now become the lightning rods and have to bear the pressures of leadership in one of the most violent businesses in the world. As Cardenas left the area his thoughts turned to the taste of champagne and beautiful women. He would not have to worry about security forces kicking down his door. At least for a while. He grinned ear to ear and put his hands behind his head and leaned back in his seat.

Alarico and Samuel, early one morning, were having huevos and machaca for breakfast when they overheard a broadcast on Univision that the Mexican Navy was going to conduct major operations on both the Pacific and Caribbean areas of the country against cocaine smuggling. It would also use the marines to patrol known drug trafficking routes, along with the army. The president wanted to stop the escalating violence in the country and knew it could only happen by impeding the flow of drugs.

Alarico declared, "Fucking president! He just can't leave well enough alone. We have to quickly develop another route. Our survival depends on the continual flow of drugs into the U.S. and cocaine is one of our most lucrative drugs. If we falter, our customers will seek other sources and then we are really fucked."

"We really should have several routes to avoid these types of problems, responded Samuel. "I have an idea! Many years ago, I met a man who is friends with Orlando Perez, the current president of Honduras. His name is Pedro Garcia and I still have his telephone number. I will call him tomorrow and see if he can arrange a meeting with Perez. He might be willing to help our activities for money of course!"

Alarico smirked, "That is great thinking, my friend! Call him when you can and see if he can hook us up with Perez. I am sure the president can be bought like most politicians. They all have a price tag."

Very early the next day, Samuel retrieved his small red telephone book and quickly found Garcia's number in Honduras. He dialed, but the international lines were busy. A few minutes later, he tried again and the call went through. Garcia answered!

Samuel declared, "Pedro, this is Samuel from Mexico. I don't know if you remember me, but we met at a bar in Guadalajara and got drunk? You were down here on vacation."

"Hey, I remember you, Samuel," shouted Garcia. "How could I forget? You kept buying me shots of tequila and I paid for it the next day. How are you, my friend?"

Samuel stated, "I am doing fine and called to ask you for a big favor. You had mentioned you knew the president of Honduras and was wondering if you could arrange a meeting with him. My partner and I would like to discuss the possibility of doing business in the country."

Garcia laughed, "My friend, of course, I will do it for you. I went to school with the president and we get together for lunch or dinner every week. Getting you a meeting will not be a problem. By the way, I am having lunch with him day after tomorrow. I have your number locked in on my phone so I will call you once it is confirmed. Take care and stay away from the tequila. My head hurts just thinking about it."

As Garcia had promised, he called two days later. The phone connections were frustrating in Mexico and Latin America because the lines were either busy or the parties on the line could not hear one another. Garcia could not hear Samuel so he hung up and redialed. The line was much better.

Garcia spoke loudly, "Samuel, the president will meet with you and your associate in two days. It will be at ten in the morning so don't be late. Good luck!"

"Thank you so much, I will not forget the favor," commented Samuel. "We will be on time. After all, the president of a country cannot be kept waiting. Hope to see you soon, my friend."

That evening, Alarico and Samuel did some research on the Honduran president. They learned he had grown up in a small village and had been a peasant farmer of coffee beans. Through political ass kissing, he had been elected into the

National Congress after graduating from the Autonomous University of Honduras where he had been a mediocre student. While in congress, he served the interests of the wealthy to the detriment of the poor. He took no interest in bettering the dismal judicial system or the security forces in the country. His brother, Antonio, was allegedly tied to the cocaine trade. Later, Perez decided to run for president and won as a result of the large donations made by his rich masters.

The following evening, Alarico and Samuel took the Lear jet belonging to the cartel and flew to Tegucigalpa, the capital city of Honduras. The flight was six hours, but Alarico and Samuel played cards and drank Dom Perignon champagne, which made the trip seem shorter. They landed at the Toncontin International Airport like a feather gently gliding onto the ground. Alarico and Samuel didn't know it was one of the most dangerous airports in the world because of its close proximity to tall, rugged mountains. Many skilled pilots had slammed into the jagged peaks scattering human cargo into rocks and trees.

A taxi was waiting and quickly whisked them away from the airport and into the crowded streets of the city. They drove by the Plaza Morazán and saw the breathtaking Cathedral of St. Michael the Archangel, which was built in the eighteenth century. Within half an hour, they arrived at the Hotel Plaza Juan Carlos, a tall, white building with blue tinted windows. After giving the cab driver a hefty tip, the two men entered the nicely appointed lobby with blue-colored sofas and tall, potted palm trees. They checked into the hotel using false Mexican passports and went to their spacious rooms. Leaving their suitcases on the bed, Alarico and Samuel met a few minutes later in the lobby. Both were hungry and walked a few blocks until they ran across the Hacienda Real Restaurant. They decided it was as good as any, so they entered the establishment with marble tiled floor and glass covered wooden tables. The chairs had plush red cushions. The two friends ordered the national dish of the country, which consisted of a huge serving of beef, plantains, red beans, marinated cabbage, fresh cream, and tortillas. To drink, they had guaro, a liquor made from distilled sugar cane juices. They only had one glass because of its overly sweet taste.

That night as a strong wind plummeted the city with dust and pollen, Alarico and Samuel sat at the hotel bar having a nightcap of high-octane Flor de Caña Rum. They were concerned with Cardenas and wondered if he would ever return. At their last meeting, he looked like a downtrodden man. The pressure was becoming too much for him. Alarico gulped down his rum and ordered another one.

Alarico, in a low voice, stated, "Samuel, when we return to Mexico, I am of the opinion we will have to make our move and seize complete power. I have heard from several of our people that Claudia and Jesus have been plotting against us. They feel they should be the ones in charge. We cannot wait until they come after us. We need to strike first and do it with complete savagery, as an example to others who may be thinking the same thing."

"I totally agree with you," responded Samuel. "I have heard the same thing about Claudia and Jesus. They may be good killers, but pulling the trigger of a gun does not make you a leader. Cardenas is pretty much washed up and suffering from severe emotional fatigue. Not a good thing in this business of ours."

Alarico and Samuel finished their drinks and decided to call it a night. They went to bed early and slept soundly with the influence of the strong alcohol.

Early the next day, the two friends showered and had baleadas for breakfast. The tortillas filled with cheese, avocados, beans, and scrambled eggs were mouthwatering. Afterwards, the men took a cab to the presidential palace, which was a pink-colored building with massive white columns in front. Large numbers of people walked in and out of the building literally bumping into one another. At a lobby reception desk, Alarico and Samuel were directed to the third floor after receiving visitor identification badges.

They entered a small elevator that creaked and sluggishly crept upwards. When the door opened, a uniformed army officer greeted them and escorted them to a waiting room with three cheap, brown sofas. Almost an hour later, the men were finally allowed into President Perez's spacious office. Behind his desk was the Honduran flag with its three horizontal bands of blue and white. It had five blue stars arranged in an X, which stood for the former federation of Honduras, El Salvador, Nicaragua, Costa Rica, and Guatemala. The short, stocky dark-skinned man in a light blue suit stood up and shook hands with Alarico and Samuel.

The president stated, "Welcome to Honduras! I was told you had something important to discuss with me. I have always been very accommodating to our northern neighbors."

"Thank you so much for being gracious enough to receive us," remarked Alarico. "We would like to donate a million dollars to your next presidential campaign for a favor."

"And pray tell what would that favor involve?" smiled President Perez. "I don't want to engage in anything, which would cause me problems."

Alarico replied, "Quite frankly, we represent the interests of the Azteca Cartel and would like to reach an agreement with you to use Honduras as a transshipment point for cocaine from Colombia. You do not need to personally involve yourself in the operations, but just ensure your security forces are not in the area when shipments are scheduled to arrive."

"I am not sure that is a wise move on my part," responded the president. "It is something I find difficultly with. Do you understand?"

Alarico then drove the point home, "Listen, we know

you make a little over four thousand dollars a month as president, which is very little money. You need to think of your retirement. Do you want to leave the presidency a rich man or a poor one? Think of our offer as a means to a better life for you and your family. We can pay you a million dollars a month. It is our final offer, take it or leave it."

President Perez was pensive and then replied, "Well, you make a very compelling argument. I am certainly not rewarded for all that I do for this country. People don't appreciate me. The hell with it. I accept your offer. When can I expect the first payment?"

"Give us the bank account information where you want it sent to and we will wire it within a week," answered Alarico. "We will also need your cell phone number so we can coordinate the movement of cocaine with you directly. Please ensure you answer our calls at all times, understand?"

The president happily commented, "Totally understand! I am so happy you came and we could reach an accommodation. This is my personal business card with the cell phone number where you can reach me twenty-four hours a day. Have a safe journey back to Mexico."

Within a week, tons of Colombian cocaine began to flow into Honduras by boat, submarine, and twin-engine aircraft. The Mosquito Coast on the eastern side of the country rapidly became a very active clandestine landing area for drug planes. The cocaine was then smuggled into Mexico through

Guatemala. Both countries had a very porous common border of almost nine hundred kilometers.

One dark night, as a strong wind whooshed through tall pine trees surrounding a ranch house sixty kilometers from Guadalajara, Claudia and Jesus arrived in a red Ford Explorer with two other sicarios. Alarico and Samuel had summoned them to a meeting. All four of them entered the house suspiciously, but were put at ease by Alarico's smile. He immediately poured them a glass of Clase Azul Anniversary Edition tequila, which cost thirty thousand dollars a bottle.

Alarico stated, "I wanted to talk with you about giving you more responsibility within the cartel. I would like for you to begin supervising all of the laboratories where we produce fentanyl. It is a big money maker for the organization and it would mean much more money for you. What do you think?"

Dressed in tight black pants and a skimpy blouse, Claudia replied sarcastically, "Fuck you! Jesus and I should be running the cartel. We have done all the dirty work and have not been recognized for our contributions. You and Samuel joined the cartel much later than we did so no, we are not going to settle for fucking scraps."

Suddenly, without warning, several men burst into the room and fired automatic bursts of gunfire from their AK-47s. Claudia, Jesus, and the other two sicarios were each shot several times. All of them died immediately, except Claudia who leaned against a wall and groaned loudly from intense pain. Blood was starting to pour out of her mouth like a river. She looked at Samuel as he approached her and said, "We knew that was going to be your answer and by doing so, you signed your own death warrants." He fired a single bullet from his handgun and it entered an inch above her left eye pulverizing her brain.

The following day, people driving into Guadalajara from the south observed four decapitated heads neatly arranged on a large wooden table. There were dead rats stuffed into their mouths. A large sign, next to the table, stated, "This is what happens to fucking traitors."

Everything was running smoothly and the Azteca Cartel, under the tutelage of Alarico and Samuel, was growing exponentially. The cartel now operated in twenty-three of the thirty-two Mexican states. It was also establishing distribution tentacles in several continents. As this unprecedented growth was taking place, Cardenas was having almost daily drunken and cocaine fueled parties attended by prostitutes. Drugs were causing him to get extraordinarily careless.

One day, one of the prostitutes appeared at a local marine garrison. She was deathly afraid of what might happen to her if she was discovered to be snitching on Cardenas. Her life would not be worth a single peso. The driving motivation was the cancer slowly consuming her mother. The money she made by selling her body only paid for food and shelter. To her, the risk was well worth it. She met with the commander of the marines and gave him the address where Cardenas was hiding.

The sun had just set when fifty marines armed with German made HK-33 assault rifles began to surround the building where Cardenas was allegedly hiding. Before they had a chance to do so, shots rang out in the quiet night and the area turned into a warzone. Bullets ricocheted on the street below as the marines ducked for cover. The soldiers began to pepper the walls of the building and people living nearby ran out of their homes into the dark night in a panic. The battle went on for over five hours until the marines called in one of their Black Hawk helicopters for operational support. It had a mounted M134 mini-gun, which was a six-barrel rotary machine gun that could fire up to six thousand rounds per minute. The marines had fired it in rural areas, but this would be the first time it would be used in an urban setting. Not long after, the helicopter could be heard approaching and it began to hover over the building where Cardenas and some of his men were on the roof shooting down on the marines. In a spectacular display of firepower, an initial thirty-second burst of thousands of rounds, in a cascading shower of light, was fired at the traffickers. Another long burst followed. The marines on the ground were in awe of the destructive nature of the mini-gun. The helicopter suddenly made a sharp turn and headed back to base after restoring an eerie silence to the night. The marines entered the building and quickly discovered the bodies of Cardenas and all of his bodyguards. They had been literally ground up like hamburger by the high velocity projectiles.

CHAPTER 8

THE BIRTH OF A NEW CAPO

After the violent death of Cardenas, Alarico consolidated his power within the cartel. No one dared question his authority and everyone fell in line like so many chess pieces. To dissent was certain and swift death. Alarico wanted to expand his empire and he knew like any wartime commander that dominating key territory was critical. In this case, it was controlling cultivation areas and significant drug routes, especially those into the U.S., but this would mean having to engage in conflict with other powerful cartels who were more treacherous than a diamondback rattlesnake. Despite the risks, Alarico knew he had to conquer more terrain in order to survive as other up and coming criminal groups became stronger.

On a warm day with clear, blue skies, Alarico held a summit meeting with his top leaders to discuss the expansion of the Azteca Cartel and to get their opinions. They all met at a ranch three kilometers from the small, picturesque village of San Juan de los Lagos located in the northeast corner of Jalisco. The men sat around a large, spectacular wooden table with infused turquoise and round geodes. It was covered with trays of lobster and shrimp. There were also several bottles of expensive tequila with crystal shot glasses strategically placed around the table.

Alarico addressed the group as they ate and drank, "I have brought you here today to discuss the growth of our cartel. I don't have to tell you we are in a deadly business, which requires vision and strategy. Status quo is nothing more than complacency and deadlier than a bullet to the head. In order to remain a powerful cartel, we need to control the primary drug routes. The most important one is the Tijuana/San Diego port of entry. Over fifty million people use it to cross over into the U.S. Our profits would go through the roof, if we control this corridor."

A tall man, in jeans and eel skin boots, stated, "Alarico, you are absolutely correct. Everyone wants that corridor, but the Tijuana Cartel controls it with an iron fist and they are not to be fucked with. They will fight to the death to keep it."

Alarico replied, "I am fully aware of that and if we have to go to war with them, so be it. If we remain as we are, other cartels will become stronger and will come after us like ravenous dogs. I have an idea on how to take the corridor away from the Tijuana Cartel. We will attack them from the south and use our friends from the Mexican Mafia to move against them from the north. They will be caught in the middle of a military style pincer movement, which, in essence, is a simultaneous strike on both their flanks. I sent an emissary to see Arturo Enriquez, the Mexican Mafia leader that Samuel and I befriended in San Quentin Prison. Although he is serving a life sentence, he has ordered his men on the outside to help us destroy the Tijuana Cartel. In return, they will be our sole drug distributors in California and Arizona. They scratch our back and we scratch theirs."

"It is a brilliant plan and now we need to do our homework," remarked Samuel. "We need to send several of our people to start collecting information on the Tijuana Cartel leaders. Intelligence on the cars they drive, where they live, businesses, associates, and the politicians who protect them. When we have this data, we will strike and erase them from the earth like they never even existed."

Alarico chimed in, "Well, you have your marching orders. Do you have any other questions?"

The men remained silent. The instructions had been given and now it was up to them to make sure they were carried out. No one wanted to engage in a war, but they knew Alarico was right. The strongest species always devoured the weakest ones and this was also very true in the evolution of drug cartels.

Within seventy-two hours, members of the Azteca Cartel began to arrive in Tijuana. It was a sprawling border city with a population of two million people and was located on the Pacific coast of Baja California. For decades, it was a growing cultural center, but it also had a seedy side. It was the base of operations for the Tijuana Cartel, which dominated the city through violence and wholesale corruption. The governor of the state, Emilio Macias, was in their pocket and he diverted state and municipal forces away from all their illicit activities. For his assistance, he was paid millions of dollars every year. Macias had become one of the wealthiest men in the country. The Tijuana Cartel trafficked cocaine, marijuana, methamphetamine and heroin in ton quantities. Their revenue was five billion dollars a year and counting. Seven brothers, belonging to the Arellano Felix family, ran the cartel.

The members of the Azteca Cartel, upon their arrival in Tijuana, began to operate in groups and they quickly identified popular nightclubs where the Arellano Felix brothers hung out and picked up women. Drunk and kissing their female companions, the powerful brothers did not notice they were being followed. With great ease, the Azteca Cartel teams were able to collect a tremendous amount of information. They also observed the Tijuana Cartel leaders meet with associates and corrupt politicians.

One hot, humid evening, they followed two of the Arellano Felix brothers, Ramon and Benjamin, to the Villa Saverios Restaurant, a five-star eatery. The brothers parked their silver Mercedes Benz in the triangle-shaped parking lot.

They took their time getting out. Benjamin was a short man who combed his hair to the side. Ramon, the lord executioner for the cartel, was stocky and had a boyish face. Both wore jeans and flamboyant Tommy Bahama shirts. After the cartel leaders went inside, two Azteca Cartel gunmen followed them. The restaurant was full of wine racks stacked against the walls and the tables had fancy white linen tablecloths. The floors were covered in expensive Italian beige marble.

Ramon and Benjamin were meeting with Governor Macias who was dressed in a black suit, white shirt and a bright pink tie. He was bald, wore stylish Italian eyeglasses, and had a well-groomed beard. They ordered expensive Armand de Brignac Brut Gold champagne with their steak and lobster. The champagne was almost seven thousand dollars a bottle. All of them were enjoying each other's company as their laughter was loud and frequent. Alarico's men had itchy trigger fingers, but the governor had too much security inside and outside the establishment. It would have been suicidal. Besides their orders were to collect information so the entire Tijuana Cartel could be crushed.

After two hours, Ramon, Benjamin, and the governor left the restaurant. Shaking hands outside, they went their separate ways. The two cartel leaders were followed to a large mansion on the southern outskirts of Tijuana. Over fifty cars were parked around the opulent residence. The sound of accordions, electric guitars, and drums blasted out into the pitch-black night. There were at least thirty men armed with assault weapons providing security. It was not until the early morning hours that everyone began to leave. Alarico's men didn't follow them, but waited patiently nearby. The sun was beginning to rise and reflect off the desert sand when an old truck left the residence. It was stopped about three kilometers away and the sole occupant, an old man with missing teeth and a scraggly beard, was abducted at gunpoint. The Azteca Cartel gunmen took him to an isolated patch of trees where he began to plead for his life.

The old man cried, "Please don't kill me. I have done nothing wrong. I have a family, which rely on me to support them. I will do anything you ask."

The leader of the Azteca gunmen calmly asked, "What is it you do at the house you just came from and who were all the people at the party? Don't lie to me or we will cut off your fucking head, understand?"

Sobbing, the old man trembled and replied, "I just take care of the place and make arrangements for food and drink to be brought in for parties. The people are all the Tijuana Cartel leaders who come every Friday night to blow off some steam. I also make arrangements for prostitutes to be available."

The gunman grilled him, "So you are saying every week the Tijuana Cartel holds a party for all its leaders? Do any politicians or government officials attend them?"

Almost hysterical, the old man responded, "Yes, all of them come. It is almost like a ritual and most often than not there are police commanders, and even army generals. I beg you to let me go. I have told you everything I know."

The gunman laughed, "You have to do one more thing. Go about your business like this never happened. Next Friday, you will arrange the party as usual. When we arrive, you will make your way out the back door and we will not harm you. Afterwards, you will just tell everyone you barely escaped the terrible massacre. If you cross us, we will kill all of your family. Do you understand?"

The old man nodded his head. He knew full well he stood a better chance of survival if he played along with the Azteca Cartel. He would have to maintain his composure and not allow his Tijuana Cartel bosses know he was going to betray them. He had just made it easier for Alarico and his people to obliterate their rivals.

Armed with the information, which had fallen into his lap, Alarico sat down with several of his cartel leaders and began to meticulously develop their plan. All of them knew they could not afford any mistakes since it could be their only chance to kill their enemies. The Mexican Mafia was also ready to join the attack, when the time came.

By Thursday morning, Alarico and Samuel along with sixty members of their cartel had arrived in Tijuana and spread across the city in different hotels. They kept a low profile and pretty much stayed in their rooms ordering room service for all their meals. All long weapons were secured in the trunks of their cars.

On Friday morning, over thirty bloodthirsty killers from the Mexican Mafia began to pour across the border from San Diego into Tijuana. They did not have to smuggle any weapons since Alarico's men brought a large panel truck full of Colt .45 semi-automatic handguns and dozens of AK-47s, which had been converted to fully automatic. For good measure, Samuel had also included a box of twenty fragmentation grenades.

That evening, teams of combined Mexican Mafia and Azteca Cartel assassins began to get into place. Many of them had to walk several miles so they could surround the house and not be detected. By the time people began to arrive at the residence, everyone was in place and radio communication was crystal clear. Alarico would take the lead and notify everyone when to strike. At almost midnight, the party was in full swing and the music rose to a crescendo. Men and women staggered out of the house to smoke and get some fresh air. Even the security guards outside were drinking and smoking joints of potent marijuana. It was not long after when the old man came out the backdoor and began to run as fast as he could.

Alarico gave the order, "Muchachos, it is time to attack all of these cabrones. Let's do it!"

Several hand grenades were hurled towards the house and the huge, fiery blasts killed several of the bodyguards and panicked the people in the house. They immediately began fleeing out the back and front of the house. A barrage of bullets mowed them down like blades of grass being cut by a lawn mower. Gunfire then erupted from within the house. Two of Alarico's men tossed grenades through the shattered windows and the blasts literally shook the house. Seconds later, the Azteca Cartel assassins moved in quickly through the rear door and more gunshots erupted, but a minute later it was all over. Alarico and Samuel entered the front door and saw mutilated bodies of men and women piled up throughout the house. Their blood was intermingled in large pools of red and it looked like the scene from a horror movie. In one of the back bedrooms, they found Ramon who was still alive, but badly wounded.

Alarico smiled at him and said, "I don't have to tell you this is the life both of us have chosen. It is dog eat dog and sooner or later you would have done the same thing to me. Just so you know, this is not personal. It is strictly business."

Ramon, grimacing in pain, replied, "Fuck you! The time will come soon enough when you too will face Santa Muerte."

Alarico pulled out his Beretta .9mm from his waistband and shot Ramon once in the forehead. Blood gushed out as his eyes rolled back in their sockets. Several Tijuana Cartel leaders were decapitated and their heads were lined up in front of the house. A white bed sheet was placed on the wall above them that read, "This is now the territory of the Azteca Cartel. We have come to protect the interests of the innocent people of Baja California against the predatory Tijuana Cartel."

The Mexican cartels had learned the significant value of using propaganda and always branded themselves as the saviors of the people and vilified their enemies as violent thugs.

During the following week, Alarico's men conducted mop-up operations in the area killing several mid and low-level Tijuana Cartel members. One day, five of his men walked into a plush restaurant where three rival cartel members were dining with their wives. They opened fire with their pistols. Bullets shattered crystal goblets and fine china on the tables. Shrieks of panic came from the patrons as the six individuals sitting in a corner table were being slaughtered. The three men and two women slumped in their chairs and though they were already dead, their bodies jerked violently as more bullets slammed into them. The third woman, of the group, had stood up and was immediately shot in the neck severing her carotid artery. Blood spurted everywhere and she put her hand over her wound trying to stop the bleeding. Two more bullets smashed into her face blowing her brains out against the nearby wall. The gunmen laughed loudly and then nonchalantly walked out.

Not more than a week later, Governor Macias was holding a political rally in Mexicali, the capital of Baja California

Norte. He stood in front of the orange colored, Cathedral of Nuestra Senora de Guadalupe addressing a large crowd speaking about his efforts to rid the state of corruption and taking the fight to the drug cartels. People cheered and clapped at his remarks. He didn't know he was giving his last political speech. Three hundred meters to the south, a man on the roof of a ten-story hotel opened a long, metal case and took out a Barrett M82 .50 caliber sniper rifle. He had been a member of Mexico's Special Forces before being recruited by the Azteca Cartel. Placing the heavy weapon on the edge of the roof, he looked through the telescopic sights and quickly had Macias in his crosshairs. His breathing became soft and shallow as he slowly began squeezing the trigger. The loud boom scared a flock of pigeons on a nearby roof and they quickly flew away shedding feathers in the process. The stock of the rifle slammed hard against the shoulder of the assassin. A second later, the large projectile smashed into Macias's face completely evaporating it into a mist of blood. People could not believe what they had just witnessed and ran from the area trampling over each other. The assassin calmly put the weapon back in the case and took an elevator to the hotel lobby. No one paid attention to him. All the hotel staff were busy registering a large group of tourists from Prescott, Arizona, who had arrived to see the bullfights the next day. The assassin was dozens of kilometers out of the city before a coordinated police response was even generated.

That evening, all the Mexican television networks reported the governor had been killed by organized crime for his unfettered attack on violence and corruption. They were unaware he had become a wealthy man from all the bribes paid to him. The Mexican president proclaimed a day of mourning and honored the governor by calling him a true patriot who had always defended his country until the very end.

Alarico and Samuel watched the newscasts as they downed shots of tequila and ate tacos al pastor. The men they commanded were consolidating the Azteca Cartels total dominance in Tijuana. They had already rented large warehouses where tons of drugs could be stored temporarily until they could be smuggled into the U.S. Over a dozen houses had been purchased outright with drug money so they could be used as safe houses for the cartel leaders when visiting the area.

Alarico sent prominent attorneys, who had extensive political contacts, to bribe public officials. They were told to either accept the money or be killed. The politicians readily took the money since they knew it would be suicide to do otherwise. Alarico also invested over three million dollars in a sizeable trucking company, which had been in business for over twenty years. It would be used to smuggle tons of drugs into the U.S. through the Tijuana/San Diego port of entry.

Alarico, one evening while watching the news on television,

received a call from one of his men, Carlos. Alarico put it on speaker so Samuel would also be privy to the conversation.

Carlos stated, "Alarico, I have some good news. A friend of mine has a distant cousin, Juan, who works for U.S. Customs and he is currently assigned to the port of entry. We all met at Juan's house in San Diego last night for a few beers. He mentioned he had two sons who wanted to go to San Diego State University, but he did not have the finances. I told him he could work for us with little risk and make a lot of money by allowing our drugs to pass safely. He has agreed to help us."

"That is very good news," Alarico stated. "I assume he is trustworthy and will not double cross us?"

Carlos replied loudly, "Yes, he can be trusted! I told him his whole family would pay the consequences if he fucked us. I guarantee, he will not do anything stupid."

Samuel commented, "Carlos, let's test his worth in the next few days. Coordinate a small load with him and let's see if he allows it to get through."

"That is a good idea," Carlos answered. "I will try to smuggle fifty kilos of cocaine in one of our cars to check him out and will get back to you, one way or the another."

Alarico then inquired, "Carlos, are you coordinating the transfer of the drugs once they cross into the U.S. with our brothers from the Mexican Mafia?"

"Of course, I am in daily contact with them," Carlos retorted. "They are doing a great job distributing our drugs throughout the entire southwestern U.S. and are now looking to expand to the eastern part of the country. As you ordered, we are keeping ledgers on all of our transactions. They are quickly funneling our profits to us in bulk cash and everything is running very smoothly."

Alarico stated, "Great, please let us know if your friend's cousin, Juan, works out. Keep us advised on any issues and we will talk soon."

Storm clouds were rapidly beginning to cover the skies over the San Diego/Tijuana area when an early model Toyota Corolla left a rustic, auto repair shop located in the center of Tijuana. The driver was an old woman who was poorly dressed in torn jeans and a tattered hoodie with the imprint of an American flag on the front. She drove slowly and got into lane seven. Vehicles were already backed up for almost a kilometer. Hordes of venders were moving between the lines of cars and trucks selling water, newspapers, religious artifacts, and wooden puppets for kids. The woman slowly inched her way forward pressing on the accelerator and brakes almost simultaneously. Eventually, she arrived at the customs booth where Juan was working. Juan looked at her and asked, "Do you have anything to declare?"

The old women looked up and meekly answered, "No, I do not. I am on my way to visit my relatives for the day."

Juan, who had been given a description of the car and license plate number the previous night was falsely told the trunk would be full of cocaine although it only contained fifty kilos. He quickly waved her through. The old woman drove to a nearby Safeway and parked the car. She left the keys on top of the left front tire. She walked a short distance and retrieved the keys of a red Chevrolet truck that had also been placed on the left tire. She smiled as she drove back into Mexico. Minutes later, two heavily tattooed Mexican Mafia members arrived and one of them drove away with the car containing the cocaine. It was rapidly distributed within forty-eight hours throughout southern California.

It was a chilly morning and Alarico's cousin, Felipe, who had helped him and Samuel after they were released from San Quentin Prison by giving them a place to live and getting them hired by the Jalisco State Police was busy making breakfast when he heard a loud knock on the door. He quickly removed a couple of tortillas and eggs from the stove and put them on the table. Felipe then scrambled to open the door. Standing there was a tall man with short hair and a pistol in his waistband. He had a large suitcase with him, which he handed to Felipe telling him it was from Alarico. The man turned and left. Perplexed, Felipe took it into his living room and unzipped it. What he saw almost made him faint. It was stuffed with easily over a million dollars. Inside was a note with two words, "Gracias, primo."

CHAPTER 9

MASSACRE ON THE BORDER

Money was pouring in hand over fist and it was beginning to be too much to launder. Alarico and Samuel were buying properties as easily as one bought various charms for a bracelet. They were stuffing millions of dollars in large plastic containers and burying them in the backyards of their properties. The walls of many of their homes were also packed with cash.

A month later, a mutual friend, at a restaurant a few kilometers south of Guadalajara, introduced them to the owner of Banco Pacifico, and after making the introduction quickly left for an appointment with his doctor. The bank was one of the largest and most prestigious in the country. Andres Montes was distinguished looking with his white hair and trimmed mustache. He wore a conservative, blue pinstripe suit and burgundy silk tie. His family had owned the bank for decades and when his father passed away from cancer, Andres took over the business. Alarico invited him to join him and

Samuel for lunch. He graciously accepted. Andres sat down and daintily put a crisp linen napkin on his lap.

Alarico opened the conversation, "So you are a banker? How is the banking business these days? It must be pretty lucrative?"

"It has its ups and downs," Andres replied. "Recently, it has not been doing well with the devaluation of the peso. Our president has made some bad decisions regarding the economy and it is impacting everyone in the country, as you know. Sadly, I had no choice but to let some of my employees go and they had been with us for many years."

Alarico feigned dismay, "That is tragic. Maybe we can help. Samuel and I own a lot of companies and have been rather lucky in getting big returns on our investments. We can give you a big boost by depositing a lot of money, in dollars, into your bank!"

Andres smiled, "Let's stop with the pretenses. You are famous drug traffickers. I have seen your photographs in the newspapers, but I am not exactly a saint either. We all have our faults. How much are you planning on depositing?"

"We will start with two hundred million dollars and once you prove to be a reliable partner, it will more than quadruple, replied Alarico. "Beware, if you double cross us, the consequences will be fatal. Not good at all, understand?"

Andres frowned and stated, "You do not have to worry about me. I am not a stupid man. When you begin putting the money in my bank, I will tell my employees, so as not to arouse their suspicions, that you are very wealthy friends of mine."

"We will start in the next two days," responded Alarico. "Samuel will meet with you at the bank and open several accounts in several fictitious names. The money will then begin to literally flood into your bank. Looks like we have a deal. Now let's all enjoy our lunch."

Two weeks later, Alarico and Samuel were in Nayarit arranging for a load of cocaine from Colombia when Alarico's cell phone rang. It was Carlos and he seemed agitated.

Carlos spoke rapidly, "Alarico, we have a problem with Juan, the U.S. Customs official who has been allowing our drugs to enter safely into America. I guess he has developed a drinking problem. Yesterday, he was supposed to be available to help us smuggle four hundred kilograms of cocaine and he never showed up for work. He was drunk. Anyway, the cocaine got seized and one of our men got arrested. Juan has become a liability to us. What do you want me to do?"

"Get rid of him," Alarico quickly responded. "We can't have a single unreliable person working for us. They can damage the cartel. It's just a matter of time before he gets arrested and I am sure he will become a rat."

Carlos replied, "I will take care of it and not make it appear it was us. We don't need the gringo law enforcement agents coming after us. It is one less distraction for us. I will contact you soon."

A week later, during a scorching hot day, Juan left his house and headed to a nearby liquor store to buy a quart of Jack Daniels. He parked his car in the empty parking lot and walked briskly to the front door wearing a blue jogging outfit and white baseball cap. He needed a drink and was focused on quenching his incessant thirst. He did not notice a bright, green panel truck follow him into the parking area. Two men wearing black ski masks covering their head and face, with only two small openings for the eyes, entered the liquor store and began shooting at Juan. The blasts from the Colt .45s reverberated loudly in the small building. Juan took two rounds to the small of his back as he tried to run. He crashed into a large display of vodka. The bottles crashed to the floor and glass shards slid across the tile. Juan looked up and saw the two men point their guns at his face. Two more explosions and he died in a large pool of expensive booze. One of the men reached into his pants pocket and retrieved a white piece of paper and placed it on Juan's bloody chest. It read, "This is for betraying the Aryan Brotherhood."

The local homicide investigators quickly held a press conference and stated it appeared to be a revenge killing by the violent, white supremacist gang. The San Diego Police public information officer advised they were investigating the possibility Juan may have been assisting the Aryan

Brotherhood to smuggle drugs into the U.S. It was almost a foregone conclusion the crime would forever go unsolved.

One morning, the peace and quiet was interrupted when the roosters began crowing loudly outside a farm twenty kilometers from Morelia, Michoacán. It was a safe house owned by the Azteca Cartel. Startled, Alarico woke up from his deep slumber. Getting out of bed, he walked over to Samuels's room and shook him by his shoulders.

"Samuel, it is time to get up," Alarico commented. "We can't be late for our meeting with General Salvador Ramirez. If we can broker a deal with him, it will make us richer beyond our wildest dreams. Get in the shower."

Forty minutes later, they were on the road to Lázaro Cárdenas, which was home to a deep-water seaport on the Pacific side of the country. It was the largest Mexican seaport and had an annual traffic capacity of over thirty million tons of cargo. It handled container and liquid cargo from different parts of the world, especially from Southeast Asia and South America. The port had both public and private terminals. The drive was very short and they quickly found the Parrilla de Casablanca Restaurant where the meeting with General Ramirez, the commander of the twenty-first military zone, was to take place. They made a slow turn into the parking lot and saw several camouflaged jeeps. Over twenty uniformed soldiers stood nearby smoking cigarettes and chatting in huddled groups. Alarico and Samuel were dressed casually in denim jeans and flowered linen shirts. They entered the dark restaurant and it took them several seconds to adjust their eyesight. The interior was painted in a subtle yellow color and potted palm trees were scattered everywhere. The tabletops were made of thick glass and wine goblets littered the top of them. The general, in full dress uniform, sat alone near an exit door. He was pale with short-cropped white hair. He had large biceps and one could tell he was in great physical shape. General Ramirez stood up from his chair and vigorously shook hands with Alarico and Samuel.

General Ramirez remarked, "I was told you are influential men who wanted to meet and discuss a potential business venture. I don't want to get into a discussion about what business since I know what it is. So, let's skip that and get into your requirements as well as mine."

"I agree with you," Alarico stated. "We need protection in bringing precursor chemicals from China to manufacture fentanyl and we will soon begin producing methamphetamine. We have been transporting chemicals through the airport in Mexico City, but it is becoming complicated since it is now swarming with all kinds of security forces. Secondly, we are growing and therefore need much greater quantities. Importing them through containerized ships is the only answer. You can protect us at this port from any police scrutiny and then help us move the tons of chemicals into our laboratories."

General Ramirez paused momentarily and then remarked,

"That is fine. I can certainly assist you, but for a fee of a hundred thousand dollars a month. I do not want pesos because they are virtually useless and fluctuate almost on a daily basis. Do we have a deal?"

Alarico smiled, "We definitely have a deal. We will pay you the first month in advance in a couple of days."

"I will give you a cell phone number I use for this type of business," retorted General Ramirez. "My code name will be "El Padrino" and you are never to use my real name in any conversation. The gringos are always monitoring telephone communications. We have to be extremely careful. I am sure you understand."

"We take many precautions," chuckled Alarico. "We would not be in business long if we were careless. What dish would you recommend at this restaurant?"

General Ramirez responded, "The imperial shrimp are the best and the rice is always cooked to perfection. Let's order since I am starved."

After a leisurely meal, Alarico and Samuel accompanied the general to the large seaport to get a feel for it. They saw numerous, huge ships stacked high with maritime containers.

General Ramirez provided a short briefing, "In 2003, the government seized the port since it was literally a pirates den for many criminal groups. You are different since you will be paying a small fee. All the cargo is moved from the port by road or rail. Kansas City Southern de Mexico provides the rail service. The company has been given a concession by the government to operate in the country. The capacity at the port is growing rapidly so the highway infrastructure running north and south is being upgraded, which should help you. My men will always be available to load the chemicals into your trucks and then provide an escort to their ultimate destination."

"Thank you for the tour," Alarico commented. "Samuel will be my point of contact with you on all matters, to include your monthly payment. Be safe!"

One of the general's men took Alarico and Samuel back to their car. They were both in high spirits since it had been a highly productive day.

That evening, while relaxing at their safe house near Morelia, Samuel received a phone call from Maria, a cousin he had grown up with. She was hysterical and sobbing loudly.

Maria yelled into the phone, "Primo, they took my little girl! We tried to cross into the U.S. near San Diego and Immigration and Customs Enforcement (ICE) caught us. The animals put us in cages and mistreated us. They did not even give us food or water. Finally, they threw me back into Mexico, but kept my little girl. I don't know what to do. Please help me! I am desperate."

Samuel replied, "Maria, I am so sorry you have gone through such an ordeal. Let me hire a good attorney in San

Diego that can help you. I will be in touch very soon. Please do not worry."

Immediately, Samuel called Stanley Goldberg, one of the top lawyers in southern California. After getting all of the details he needed from Samuel, the high-priced attorney stated he would get on the case right away. He informed Samuel that child separation had become a horrible racist policy to dissuade undocumented immigrants from entering the U.S.

The next day, Goldberg called Samuel and advised he had contacted the local ICE office and was incredulous they didn't know where Maria's child was at. Their records only showed she had been sent to Miami and then had just disappeared. Goldberg told Samuel this was more than reminiscent of Nazi Germany than the U.S. He assured Samuel he would continue to pursue the case to the end. Goldberg added ICE was a racist organization and was putting migrants in cages like they were animals. It was deplorable.

One night, as the stars shined with a bright, shimmering light, Samuel and Alarico were on a computer at one of their homes in Guadalajara. They were researching the latest in weaponry and by mere chance got into a dark website advertising drone technology. They watched a video with great curiosity on killer drones the size of a man's palm. The drones flew themselves based on artificial intelligence and its sensors reacted one hundred times faster than the human brain. They had cameras, sensors, social media applications, and could target human beings based on facial recognition and other information. It was a smart weapon that consumed data making them extremely deadly. The drones had stochastic motion to protect it from sniper fire. It was the perfect weapon. A video showed they could penetrate buildings, cars, and trains if properly programmed. They carried a shaped charge of three grams of explosives and when targeting a human, the small blast would penetrate the skull and destroy the brain. The drones were highly surgical in the way they killed.

The following morning, Samuel, through the dark web, contacted a company located just south of Beijing, China and ordered three hundred of the drones. In minutes, he transferred half a million dollars to the company's bank account. Four days later, the drones arrived by air at the Guadalajara International Airport. The customs inspectors opened the boxes and assumed they were children's toys. They were dead wrong!

Samuel was raving mad about the terrible ordeal his cousin, Maria, was going through and now wanted revenge. He contacted his Mexican Mafia associates in southern California and requested their help. He asked them to go to the large ICE office in San Diego, early the next day, so they could take photos of all the employees when they arrived. Samuel also requested pictures of the ICE building as well. Twenty-four hours later, Samuel received slightly over a hundred photos on his cell phone. He immediately had one of his tech savvy people program a hundred and fifty of the killer drones to attack their targets using the photos taken by the Mexican Mafia.

Four days later, on a foggy morning, Customs and Border Protection (CBP) picked up a suspect aircraft on radar crossing the border from Tijuana into San Diego and moved rapidly to launch a Blackhawk helicopter to intercept. By the time the helicopter was revving up its engines a single engine Piper Cherokee Challenger airplane circled three thousand feet above the ICE building. The passenger opened his window and dropped the killer drones from a cardboard box. In a swarm, they dropped rapidly and their sensors quickly focused on the ICE building. One of the drones blew out a large window allowing the cluster of drones to quickly enter the building like agitated bees. In mere seconds, they began finding their human targets and explosions could be heard, which created massive panic. Two ICE agents in frumpy suits ran down a narrow hallway, but were unable to outrun the fast-moving drones, which slammed into the back of their heads turning their brains into mushy liquid. The agent in charge, a devout white supremacist, heard screaming and came out of his office to see what all the commotion was about. Two drones quickly locked in on his face and with great speed slammed into his forehead. The shaped charges went off simultaneously sending him backward onto the floor. His green eyes gazed at the ceiling and his open mouth drooled saliva onto the floor. He was on the super highway to hell. The ICE building looked like a disheveled morgue with dead bodies scattered everywhere. By the time the CBP helicopter reached the area, the suspect aircraft had long crossed the border back into Mexico. The Department of Homeland Security began an investigation along with the FBI, but neither one of them were able to develop any significant leads. The crime scene only yielded small fragments of the killer drones. The pieces were so small they could not obtain fingerprints. They were fully aware anyone who could pull off such an operation would not be foolhardy enough to leave prints that could be traced.

Three weeks later, Samuel received a call from attorney Goldberg with exciting news. He had threatened ICE with a law suit and forced them to disclose that Maria's little girl had been placed in an orphanage in Atlanta, Georgia. He made arrangements for the child to be transported to San Diego and would personally meet her at the airport. Samuel was elated and told him there would be a hefty bonus waiting for him.

After his call with Goldberg, Samuel called Maria and gave her the information he had just received. Maria was elated and thanked Samuel profusely for his help. Samuel, however, had not finished with ICE. He had developed a tremendous hatred for the racist organization.

It was an overcast day and the wind was blowing sand into the air like pellets from an air gun. Alarico and Samuel were inspecting one of their fentanyl labs near the small village of San Cristóbal de la Barranca, Jalisco, when Samuel received a call from a Mexican Mafia leader in California. He was advised that Chad Lobo, head of the U.S. Department of Homeland Security (DHS) was coming to Calexico, California, the following week to inspect the border wall being constructed. ICE was a department under DHS. Samuel, who was still angry about the situation with Maria, was driven by animalistic savagery. The head of DHS was a complete political hack, not at all suited for his position. He was a lobbyist by trade, but a pliable political moron for the president. He loved to take photos of himself wearing aviator sunglasses and a helicopter helmet. He also enjoyed creating the illusion, primarily through Fox News, of being a tough guy. He was anything, but that! Samuel knew he was one of the architects of the American child separation policy.

The following week, after inspecting part of the border wall, Lobo was having a late lunch with some of his underlings at the Diez Milpas Restaurant. They were having green chili chicken enchiladas and complimenting each other on the building of the racist wall, which anyone with common sense knew it was completely useless. The officials did not notice two men wearing expensive blazers and silk shirts enter the establishment. As they passed the table with the DHS officials, the two men turned abruptly and began shooting with .45 caliber semi-automatic handguns. In less than three seconds, all of the men lay dead with their blood draining onto the floor. People in the restaurant quickly ran out and left the area as fast as their cars would take them. One of the assassins walked up to Lobo and put a spherical, fourteen-ounce M-67 fragmentation grenade in his mouth and pulled the pin. The assassins had just cleared the building when the explosive device went off shattering the large windows. Glass shards flew everywhere covering the street in front.

ICE agents along the Mexican border began to call in sick and operations ground to a standstill. None of them needed a crystal ball to disclose they were targets of an invisible enemy. A feeling of dismay and frustration permeated the entire agency since they could not attack an enemy not yet identified. They were now the victims and not the predators of defenseless children.

A week later, three U.S. Border Patrol vehicles, with three agents in each one, were driving along the border wall looking for undocumented migrants. They stopped near a section of the racist barrier to have some water and chat. The agents soon began making jokes of the "wetbacks" they had tortured by waterboarding them.

Suddenly, tons of explosives went off along a half mile stretch of the wall, which literally vaporized the agents and knocked down a large chunk of the structure. Within a week, many DHS personnel were looking for new jobs in the private sector. Preferably hundreds of miles away from the Mexican border.

CHAPTER 10

CONQUERING MORE TERRITORY

One evening, after dinner and a few shots of expensive tequila, Alarico went to a hall closet of the house he and Samuel were staying at and pulled out a large, detailed map of Mexico. He carefully spread it out on the dining room table. He called Samuel over.

Alarico commented, "Samuel, I have been thinking of being a little more strategic in the way we do more things. I want to take control of the state of Tamaulipas, which as you know has a common border with Texas. It is an ideal area for us, especially the city of Matamoros, which borders Brownsville. Matamoros depends heavily on the international trade with the U.S. It has the Veterans International Bridge, a corridor for overweight trucks. It also has the West Rail Bridge, which is a railway crossing into the U.S. Two more significant things come to mind. One, it is only nine hundred and eighty-six kilometers from Guadalajara to Matamoros. On the other hand, it is two thousand two hundred kilometers from Guadalajara to Tijuana. A shorter route is always safer. Obviously, we will continue to use Tijuana, but we need to develop more secure routes. Secondly, direct access to the state of Texas facilitates the movement of our drugs to both the eastern and western seaboards of the U.S. This is vital to our operations that continue to expand dramatically. Don't you agree?"

Samuel was reflective and responded, "Alarico, you know it means we have to engage in yet another war since the Cartel del Noreste controls the area. It came into existence because of heavy infighting between competing elements of the Zeta Cartel when their leaders were either captured or killed. They are well armed and use armored vehicles. The cartel has a very large armed wing called the "tropa del infierno" (troops from hell). They are a force to be reckoned with."

"What is the name of their leader?" asked Alarico. "I know it will not be easy, but nothing in this business is a walk in the park. Let's prepare our best sicarios and start sending them into the area. Make sure they take enough weapons and ammunition. Give them sufficient money to live on for several months."

Samuel replied, "The leader of the cartel is Juan Gerardo Treviño. He is the nephew of Miguel Angel Treviño, the psychopath who was the former leader of the Zetas. Both of them are sadistic killers. Fortunately for us, Miguel Angel is in prison and he will be there for the rest of his life. Juan

Gerardo's favorite pastime is dismembering and decapitating people. Blood excites him like most men get excited over a beautiful woman. Juan Gerardo is a short, stocky man and has a military style crew cut. He will be one of the most dangerous predators we will ever face."

Alarico only smirked and inquired, "You mentioned they use armored vehicles. What kind are you referring to since there are so many?"

"The Cartel del Noreste is pretty much a paramilitary force," explained Samuel. They wear black uniforms and their trucks are armored with three-inch steel plates. They have men who cut the metal plates with torches and then cover their trucks with them. They also make holes on the side panels using them as gun portals to shoot at their enemies. The small windows in front are made from thick bulletproof glass, which allow the driver to see where he is going. They are virtually military tanks."

"These armored vehicles must have a weakness," commented Alarico. "Are the tires also protected by steel plates?"

Samuel responded, "Now that you mention it, no they are not. I have seen many videos on the news of the armored trucks they use and have never seen any with plates protecting the tires."

"Well, now we have our answer," smiled Alarico. "They are deadly as long as they are mobile, but are useless if they are at a standstill. Make sure our men take several rocket propelled grenades and other explosives. Let's move forward with our plan."

Within days, Azteca Cartel sicarios began to create a large presence in and around Matamoros. It did not take long before the Cartel del Noreste began to realize the rival cartel was beginning to encroach on their turf. They were not going to have any of it.

The blood red sky loomed on the horizon as leaders of the local cartel began to arrive at a large ranch just south of the city. After all of them were present, Treviño addressed the group as they sat around a large rustic table with a white and brown cow skin under it. Hanging from the roof was a chandelier made of elk horns.

In a solemn manner, Treviño stated, "As all of you know the Azteca Cartel has started coming into our area. Many of our sources have provided intelligence and now we have no choice, but to go to war with them. We are not going to be pushed out of our area, which we have dominated for years. Prepare your men and let's start killing these dogs wherever we find them."

It was not long after that the Cartel del Noreste received information that at least twenty gunmen from their deadly rivals were holed up in a house thirty kilometers west of Matamoros. Rapidly, they mobilized and set off in that direction. The large convoy consisted of three armored trucks and ten black SUVs that were not bulletproof. The SUVs had C.D.N. in large white letters on the doors. The acronym of the Cartel del Noreste. They moved at a slow pace because of the steel plated trucks. The fifty heavily armed men in the vehicles were ready for war. They were somber during the drive. Five kilometers from the location, the road narrowed into two lanes and became extremely rough. Potholes were everywhere, some half a meter deep. It slowed the convoy even more.

As they passed a grove of trees, the sharp rattle of gunfire echoed throughout the area. Rocket propelled grenades struck the tires of the armored trucks, which stopped the entire convoy. Within seconds, improvised explosive devices hidden in the potholes exploded with a deafening roar viciously tearing through the unprotected underbellies of the trucks. The vehicles were tossed a few feet in the air and violently rolled over on their sides. The explosions crushed the occupants. The SUVs were enveloped in wave after wave of AK-47 and .50-caliber machinegun fire. The lead projectiles slammed against metal and human flesh. Several Cartel del Noreste members were able to get out of their vehicles despite the withering fire and took cover in a small ditch on the side of the road. They began to lay down suppression fire, but were quickly overwhelmed. Weapons were soon tossed out into the road and men could be heard yelling they were surrendering. Six men were immediately taken prisoner. They were brutally kicked and punched until they were bleeding profusely from the nose and mouth. Their hands were bound tightly with rope and then the men were pushed down to their knees.

One of the Azteca Cartel leaders stood in front of them and looked each one in the eye. He looked like he had been in fights all his life based on all the visible scars on his face. The prisoners cowered before him.

He addressed them, "Hijos de puta! You are going to give me information and give it to me quickly. I want to know where we can find your fucking boss, Treviño. His days are numbered so you will just be hastening his death by a few days. Where is that coward?"

One of the younger prisoners spoke up, "He changes locations constantly, but he spends a lot of time at a ranch called "San Miguel" located on the main road forty kilometers south of Matamoros. There is a big sign next to the road with a rustic painting of a black horse. As you pass the sign, you will immediately see a dirt road on the right. It will take you to the ranch."

Seconds later, the prisoners were riddled with bullets. They were in grotesque positions with their faces twisted in the horror of their final seconds of life. The cartel wars were much more savage and violent than conventional warfare. They were brutal and remorseless. Drug trafficking organizations wanted to make examples of their enemies by dismembering and beheading them. The Mexican population was traumatized by the monstrosity of the cruelty. In Mexico there were more people buried in unmarked graves than those in cemeteries.

The Azteca Cartel gunmen were speeding towards the ranch where they hoped to find Treviño. They dodged slow traffic and soon encountered a man in a truck who was suffering from road rage and began yelling at the sicarios. He pulled up alongside one of their cars and was about to say something when he was shot several times in the face with an automatic AR-15. His truck went off the road and crashed into a large pine tree. Seconds later, it caught fire and was quickly incinerated.

In about an hour, the cartel gunmen arrived at the ranch. They parked their vehicles a hundred meters from the road and walked up the steep hill. Hiding behind trees and large bushes, they were able to observe about eight men standing in front of the house. They appeared to be telling jokes since there were constant eruptions of laughter. Without a care in the world, they continued their banter and didn't notice several men crawling towards them. When the gunmen were about twenty meters away, they opened fire killing all eight in the first volley. Seconds later, the front door of the house was kicked in, but a search revealed it was empty. Then they cautiously made their way to a large barn near the back of the house. The door had a thick chain with a massive padlock. One of the gunmen blasted it open with his AK-47. They were shocked to see over fifty women sitting in the dirt. They were dirty and looked like they were half-starved. They told the gunmen all of them were from Guatemala, El Salvador, and Honduras. Seeking a better way of life, they were trying to get to the U.S., but were intercepted by the Cartel del Noreste, which intended to sell them to sex trafficking merchants in the next few days. The leader of the sicarios contacted Alarico on his cell phone.

He advised, "Jefe, we hit a location owned by the Cartel de Noreste looking for that dog Treviño. He was not here, but we found fifty women from Central America, which they planned to sell into the sex trade. They were trying to get to the U.S. What do you want us to do?"

Alarico replied, "I want you to get them there. You can put them up in some of our properties in the U.S. until they can get on their feet. Treat them nice and give them money for food and clothes. We are criminals, but not animals. I do it in memory of my poor beloved mother. Take care of it right away and keep looking for that bastard Treviño."

Days later, two Azteca Cartel sicarios were told by an old man they met at a local bar that the entire Matamoros Police Department was protecting their rivals. He stated that Geronimo Herrera, the police chief, was being paid a lot of money each month for his services and had built a large mansion, which everyone called the "casa de corrupcion." He offered to show them where the house was located for a few hundred pesos. The three men drove to the most affluent area in the city and the old man pointed out a large, two-story house with rose gardens in front. A black Mercedes Benz was parked in the driveway. The sicarios took the old man back to the bar and handed him a wad of pesos. He smiled and walked into the establishment to continue the only merriment he had in life.

The sun was peering over the horizon and a soft wind moved slowly through the area. Matamoros police officers were beginning to arrive at their headquarters located in a brown box-like building with massive antennas on the roof. The parking lot was full of blue and white police cruisers. No one could have anticipated what happened next. Truckloads of Azteca Cartel gunmen arrived and quickly parked in front of the police station. Like mountain lions they leaped from their vehicles with AK-47s and AR-15s in hand. They pushed the doors open and began to shoot anyone who came into their sight. The explosions from their guns made everyone jump behind desks and chairs in a futile attempt to hide. Panic set in and the police officers and secretaries then tried to get out the doors, but bullets were flying everywhere and they died on top of each other. The gunmen found Herrera hiding in a closet. He was hit hard in the face with the wooden stock of an AK-47 and he spit out several bloody teeth on the floor. The police chief looked up as one of the gunmen put the barrel of his weapon in his mouth. The last thing he heard was a loud bang before the hot projectile ripped apart his gray matter. Blood flowed everywhere. The gunmen went from body-to-body pumping more bullets into them to make sure they had all gone into the afterlife. While this was going on, a massive explosion shattered Herrera's mansion. It was now a pile of rubble. Fortunately, Herrera's wife and three children were away visiting relatives in Ciudad Victoria.

The Azteca Cartel began moving large quantities of drugs through Matamoros into Texas and then to cities across the U.S. It was not without peril since the Cartel del Noreste was still a force to be reckoned with.

One night, as a full moon illuminated the area, a tractor-trailer carrying half a ton of fentanyl approached Matamoros. It bore Jalisco license plates. As it entered the city, several pick-up trucks and SUVs blocked the road. Several men, wearing masks and carrying assault rifles, stood nearby. They menacingly ordered the two men out of the truck and then executed them without warning. Next to the bodies a narco-manta was placed warning the Azteca Cartel that they were not welcome in the city. One of the armed men jumped into the eighteen-wheeler and drove away with its valuable cargo.

Alarico and Samuel were soon notified of the situation and they were more than homicidal. The leaders gave instructions to their men in Matamoros to intensify the hunt for the men involved in the theft. The order was to take them alive and apply torture to determine where the fentanyl had been taken.

Time was of the essence, and it needed to happen before the Cartel del Noreste moved it across the border and gave it to their U.S. distributors.

The next evening, Alarico's men followed two rival gunmen to the El Alazan Bar. They took positions around the entire establishment and waited. Three long hours passed when they saw the men come out and stagger towards their car. Tires screeched loudly and three intimidating sicarios sprang from a black sedan. They pointed handguns at the two individuals and quickly herded them into the trunk of their car. In minutes, they were on an isolated dirt road and eventually parked near a field of tall cottonwood trees. The two men in the trunk were thrown violently from the car into the dirt and kicked in the process.

An Azteca Cartel sicario asked, "Cabrones, what have you done with the fentanyl you stole from us? Start talking if you value your miserable lives."

The younger of the prisoners spoke, "We don't know what you are talking about. We had nothing to do with it. You have the wrong people."

That led to a savage beating and one of the sicarios retrieved a chicharra (electric cattle prod) from the car. They ripped the clothes from the prisoners. The prod was then applied to their genitalia, which caused excruciating pain. The shrieks from the men were deafening and their bodies stiffened when the piercing electrical charge flowed through their bodies.

The torture continued for several minutes. Finally, the older prisoner who was obese and not used to pain yelled for them to stop.

"I will tell you what you want to know," he cried. "The fentanyl is at a small ranch not far from here. The plan is to move it into the U.S. tomorrow morning so you will have to move quickly. I will take you to where the fentanyl is located as long as you promise not to kill me."

He was told he would be set free in return for his cooperation. The younger man was shot several times in the head and then run over as the sicarios turned around on the narrow road. They sped down the road leaving a cloud of dust behind them. In less than half an hour, the sicarios met up with other Azteca Cartel gunmen who would help in the attack to recover the fentanyl.

Not much later, they approached a small, rustic ranch with a cornfield to the right. Three horses were in a corral next to it and they stared at the cars as they snaked their way up the rolling hill. Explosive gunfire suddenly broke out interrupting the quiet night. The whining sound of bullets flying indiscriminately was loud. And men yelling obscenities at each other was even louder. Minutes later, four Cartel del Noreste guards were dead. The Azteca Cartel gunmen entered the unkempt house and in a back bedroom found the pile of fentanyl and an added bonus of a ton of cocaine in burlap bags. They hurriedly loaded their vehicles with the drugs and then tossed the bodies of the dead guards into the house and poured a few gallons of gasoline and set it on fire. It went up in flames like a tinderbox.

Cartel wars are like any conflict and they have a tendency to escalate rather than deescalate. The killings continued unabated between the Azteca Cartel and the Cartel del Noreste. The latter was losing men by the dozens so they began to intensify their recruitment of poor young men from the barrios who were enticed by the allure of becoming rich. It was their only escape from a vicious cycle of poverty.

With yellow streetlights shining down on them, two of Alarico's men sat in a black Dodge truck drinking beer near the main plaza in Matamoros. They were drunk and whistled out their windows at the young girls passing by. They were about to leave when three men wearing masks approached them from behind. Several shots rang out and blood spattered with great force against the windows. The killers then ran off into the night.

The following morning, the governor of the state told reporters the violence was out of hand and therefore, he had requested assistance from the Mexican army. That Saturday, several camouflaged military trucks rolled into Matamoros as curious inhabitants looked on. The commander of the military force was General Fernandez who happened to be best friends with General Ramirez, the protector of the Azteca Cartel in the state of Michoacán. Not long after, a meeting was arranged by General Ramirez between Alarico, Samuel, and General Fernandez. The leaders of the Azteca Cartel flew into the General Lucio Blanco International Airport located in Reynosa, Tamaulipas, which was only ninety-two kilometers from Matamoros. After renting a car, they drove to the La Fogata de Reynosa Restaurant. The establishment was painted white and had several arches supported by brown columns. When Alarico and Samuel entered the front door, a short man with thick white hair waved them over. He was dressed in civilian clothing.

General Fernandez stated, "You don't need to introduce yourselves. I know who you are. My good friend General Ramirez asked me to help you with the problems you are having with the Cartel del Noreste. They are a bunch of cabrones who need to be exterminated and I will be the one to do it. They killed my uncle a few years ago because he got into a bar fight with one of those savages."

"I know if we join forces, we can eliminate those putos, once and for all," Alarico commented. "We are not so much about violence; our main objective is to make money on the blood of the gringos who have fucked Mexico for over a century. We will pay you well for your troubles."

"All I ask is the same amount of money you are paying my good friend, General Ramirez" replied the general. "It will be worthwhile to you and your enterprise. I will ensure my men only attack your rivals and leave you alone. Here is my cell phone number in case you need to reach me."

While eating steak and lobster, the three men made small talk, and quickly connected with one another. Later, they exited the restaurant separately and went in different directions.

Less than three days later, General Fernandez received information from an informant that several Cartel del Noreste members were undergoing treatment in a drug rehabilitation center in Matamoros. Apparently, they had been sampling the merchandise and became heavily addicted to cocaine. The general quickly gathered some of his men and proceeded to the center, which was located in an isolated area. The building stood alone and the closest structure was a kilometer away. The soldiers piled out of their trucks and surrounded it. The general went in the front door with a group of his men and roughly pushed aside the medical personnel who meekly protested their entry. The soldiers herded all the patients into a large room and ordered them to sit quietly on the floor.

General Fernandez stared at them with a sinister look, "How many of you are with the Cartel del Noreste? You had better tell me or else all of you will pay. Do I make myself clear?"

The forty men stared blankly, but did not respond. They were transfixed on the general. The silence was deafening for five minutes. The general smirked and nodded to his soldiers. A dozen AR-15s erupted into repetitive blasts as bullets sprayed the drug addicts. Large amounts of blood splashed against the walls along with pieces of flesh. Those who were still alive were killed with Colt .45 semi-automatics at pointblank range. The soldiers turned and slowly left the building. Loud screams could be heard from the treatment facility personnel who peeked into the room. It looked like a scene from the deepest depths of hell.

A day later, the military conducted a raid at a Cartel del Noreste training camp for sicarios located at a ranch between Matamoros and Reynosa. General Fernandez moved in with over a hundred men in armored personnel vehicles with mounted .50 caliber machineguns. An hour-long firefight ensued and bullets bounced everywhere. A sicario fired a rocket-propelled grenade, which exploded in the middle of three soldiers killing them all. The machinegun fire eventually took a heavy toll on the sicarios and a few were able to escape through thick foliage located on the west side of the training compound.

Hours later, after the assault on the cartel training compound, gunmen from the Azteca Cartel in Matamoros blew up four pharmacies and a large movie theater belonging to Treviño using dynamite. Dozens of people were killed and thick smoke cast a dark shadow over Matamoros.

Almost simultaneously, another group of Azteca Cartel gunmen parked their black SUVs on a small hill overlooking a brown house with a red tiled roof. The order was given, and the sicarios charged down the hill with the precision of a skilled military unit. Closer to the house they broke off into two groups. One covered the back of the residence and the other kicked in the front door. Inside, one of the top leaders of the Cartel del Noreste was having lunch with his wife and three adult sons. They screamed as they saw the AK-47 wielding gunmen enter the dining room. It was too late. A barrage of bullets tore them into pieces. Blood covered the mashed potatoes and turkey on the table.

The army and the Azteca Cartel decided to start destroying the infrastructure of the Cartel del Noreste by going after anyone who supported them. On a chilly, rainy day, five gunmen burst into a prestigious law firm, which represented Cartel del Noreste members and methodically went from office-to-office assassinating over five attorneys and all their staff. Fifteen in total.

Six days passed and several sicarios went into an accounting firm, which helped launder money for the local cartel. They fired on employees and ordinary citizens who happened to be present. Well-placed explosives by the Azteca Cartel turned the building into dust.

One afternoon, Israel Montez, the mayor of Matamoros decided to go for a stroll near the Our Lady of Refuge Cathedral (Catedral de Matamoros), the main Catholic temple in the city. He loved the neoclassic architecture with the arches in front, which were flanked by Tuscan columns. He and his family attended mass there, without fail, every Sunday. Montez had been one of the political facilitators that had allowed the Cartel del Noreste to take control over the city. He stopped to buy a small cup of cherry ice cream from a pushcart vendor and then sat down on a wooden bench to enjoy it. Three sicarios approached him from behind and put several bullets into the back of his head. Montez pitched forward into the concrete with the plastic spoon still in his mouth. The ice cream vendor panicked and tried to flee, but his cart overturned and he tripped over it. When he looked up, he was staring at a very big handgun and the barrel looked as big as a cannon. The sicario laughed and lowered his pistol. He threw several peso notes at the old man. The three sicarios walked away giggling loudly. The vendor then passed out from abject fear.

The cartel war continued to become more deadly and people became increasingly scared they could get caught in a crossfire as the cartels battled it out in the streets. Bullets and shrapnel pockmarked many of the buildings in Matamoros. Families began to send their children to stay with relatives in other Mexican states in an effort to keep them safe.

One night, two men staggered out of the Gallo Prieto Cantina with prostitutes they had picked up. Both had been drinking Mescal since mid-day and they were feeling no pain. The men were Treviño's uncles on his father's side. They howled into the night air with glee and held on tight to the prostitutes who were squeezed into dresses several sizes too small. The women slapped the men's hands away as they tried to grope them.

One of the prostitutes yelled, "Cabrones, don't touch the merchandise. You have not paid for it yet. Pinches animales!"

One of the men tripped and fell on the street and had to be picked up. He yelled obscenities and continued to stagger forward. They were headed to a third-rate hotel located three blocks away. Suddenly, a dark gray Suburban turned the corner and skidded to a stop five meters away from the small group and three men jumped out brandishing Beretta 9mm handguns. They quickly emptied their guns on the two men who tried to run, but were too inebriated. Several bullets slammed into their backs. With all the Mescal in their system it is questionable if they felt any pain. The sicarios walked calmly back to their vehicle.

One of the prostitutes yelled, "Putos, you could have waited until we got paid."

A sicario responded, "Just take their fucking wallets!"

The next day, Treviño walked across the international bridge into Brownsville, Texas, and surrendered to the DEA. He had decided it was only a matter of time before the Azteca Cartel killed him. He did not relish being in prison, but at least he would be among the living. In less than two months, he was convicted in federal court on several charges of conspiracy, drug trafficking, and murder charges. He was sentenced to life in prison. Matamoros was now entirely in the hands of Alarico and the Azteca Cartel.

CHAPTER 11

THE FALL OF A GENERAL

Miguel Villa, the Special Agent in Charge of the Drug Enforcement Administration (DEA) in Albuquerque, New Mexico, was confronting a spike in the availability of illegal drugs, especially methamphetamine and heroin throughout the state. Law enforcement agencies were being overwhelmed and deaths from overdoses kept increasing in a dramatic manner. The drugs all had one source, the Azteca Cartel based in Mexico. The killings were also getting worse as local street gangs battled it out, in rural and urban areas, for control of territory in order to expand their drug distribution. The Azteca Cartel supplied all three hundred gangs in the Land of Enchantment and didn't care what happened between them as long as they got their money.

The U.S. Attorney for the District of New Mexico, Lillie Montoya, did not have nearly enough prosecutors on her staff to handle all of the cases ranging from white-collar crime, drug trafficking, fraud, alien smuggling and many others.

Her office was located in the old federal courthouse building in downtown Albuquerque. Every morning, she would get up before sunrise and drive sixty miles from Santa Fe into the city and not return home until late at night. It was taking a toll on her and all her staff. She had a Zoom meeting, early one Monday morning, with the fourteen district attorneys and their deputies throughout the state.

She opened the conference and remarked, "Greetings everyone! I am pleased you could join me today on an issue of grave importance. As you are all aware, the state is in a terrible crisis. Illicit drugs and violence are tearing us apart and our prosecutorial resources are stretched to the breaking point. I do not have enough prosecutors to even handle half of the cases we currently have. Therefore, I want to strike a deal with all of you. I would like to forward some cases to you that we are unable to deal with so that criminals can at least be tried in state court."

One of the district attorneys from Las Cruces replied, "I think everyone will agree with me that we can work with you on this matter. We cannot allow criminals who commit heinous crimes just to walk free. Please count on us."

U.S. Attorney Montoya breathed a sigh of relief, "Thank you everyone and we will be in contact. Have a wonderful day!"

A week later, the DEA brought her an affidavit for a Title III wire intercept requesting authorization to monitor the cellular telephone of a known Azteca Cartel leader, Daniel

Silva, who headed a large cell operating in Santa Fe, the state capital of New Mexico. The affidavit had all the prerequisites needed to get approval, i.e., complete identification of the target telephone, subject of investigation, predicate offenses, which in this case was drug trafficking, goals of investigation, and most importantly, probable cause. It also contained a statement that normal investigative procedures had been attempted and failed.

The lengthy affidavit was thoroughly reviewed by U.S. Attorney Montoya who subsequently presented it to a federal judge along with a letter from the U.S. Attorney General authorizing her to sign off on the document. The judge was so impressed with all of the probable cause, and quickly signed it.

Within a few days, Silva's cell phone was being monitored. The wire intercept room at the DEA office was in full swing. Wire intercepts were always labor intensive and quite costly, but usually yielded results since criminals had to communicate with one another and were usually too lazy to take the time and effort to meet in person. They tried to talk in code, but it was not very sophisticated and could easily be understood. At the onset, Villa met with his case agents, Mike Parra, Ed Tanuz, Lupe Martinez, and Bert Flores.

Villa stated, "I am optimistic this wire intercept is going to give us an edge on curbing much of the drug trafficking in our state along with the violent gang warfare that is taking place. The Azteca Cartel based in Mexico has undeniably become the most powerful criminal organization in the world. It is almost more powerful than the Mexican government itself. They are corrupters and now they have established roots in our state. We need to move aggressively and smartly and we are certainly up to the challenge."

Parra commented, "They are like a deadly cancer, which threatens to destroy our youth and the social fabric of our country. Our politicians don't provide much help toward our effort."

"I totally agree," Villa replied. "We have to remember that most politicians are put into office by popular vote, very much like prom queens in high school. Most are lacking in common sense and once they get into office, they become parrots that chirp their party line. They are the biggest impediments to our mission. Our illustrious U.S. congressmen and senators, every few months, have town hall meetings in the state to talk about the drug problem, but never offer any solutions or resources."

Tanuz chimed in, "I heard the governor is proposing to legalize marijuana, which is going to be a big problem for the state."

Villa smiled and stated, "Ed, you are correct. It underscores my opinion of politicians being morons. The state has one of the biggest drug problems and property crime rates in the country and this will only exacerbate our conundrum. It will create a mess of their own doing and then in the end we will have to clean it up.

Martinez inquired, "We are understaffed. Are you looking at getting us some support on the wire intercept?"

"Glad you asked that question," Villa answered. "I have spoken with Lieutenants Chris Valdez and Dominic Casados from the New Mexico State Police about working with us. They have assigned some of their best officers, Chris Quintana, Migel (not the normal spelling of Miguel) Flores, Emmanuel Rodriquez, and David Gil. As a matter of fact, they will be here tomorrow. I have already made arrangements to have them deputized as DEA task force agents. Before you ask, they will be in plainclothes so they won't stand out during surveillances or operations."

The following day, Quintana, Flores, Rodriquez, and Gil arrived at the DEA office and were sworn in by Villa and given similar looking badges as those carried by the DEA agents. They were now part of the team that would pursue the most significant cartel on the planet.

The wiretap on Silva's phone quickly became very active. All conversations were in Spanish. Most of the calls were going to and coming from the interior of Mexico. It soon became evident the Azteca Cartel was distributing ton quantities of fentanyl, methamphetamine, heroin, cocaine, and marijuana throughout the U.S., including New Mexico.

It was late Wednesday, when an incoming call was

intercepted from the state of Jalisco. It was from a man who was later identified as Juan Patron, a major player in the Azteca Cartel.

Patron stated, "Compadre, how are things where you are at? I would like to go visit you sometime soon. I understand the señoritas there are very nice. We want to send you some leather huaraches in the immediate future, but I will let you know."

Silva replied, "Pinche compadre, come and visit so we can get some chica's and drink some good tequila. The huaraches sound good since I need a new pair. How are things down there?"

Patron sighed loudly, "We have been getting into wars if you know what I mean. Surely, you have seen it on gringo television. Fortunately, we have won them all. I will call you soon when the package is on its way."

Quintana and Flores who monitored the call told Villa that something was brewing regarding a possible shipment of drugs. The DEA continued to listen to the calls and waited patiently like birds of prey.

It was a stunning red/orange sky as the sun began to set on the horizon when Rodriquez and Gil overheard an incoming call from Gregorio Chavez, the violent leader of the Los Reyes del Norte gang based in Albuquerque. It was the largest in the state and had been linked to dozens of murders. He was calling Silva and the phone rang several times before it was answered.

Chavez yelled into the phone, "Daniel, what the fuck are you doing, bro? I am running short of the tequila you gave me last month. I need twenty more bottles!"

"You are really putting it away and that is a good thing," Silva responded. "The price is the same. I will send one of my friends to take you the bottles. He can meet you in front of the Dollar Store on Central Avenue. My friend will be driving a green BMW SUV. He will meet you there in three hours. Make sure you have the money."

Chavez replied, Claro, I will have the money! We will be on time and I will be in touch soon. Take care!"

Armed with the information gleaned from the wire intercept, Villa and his men got ready. Within an hour they were positioned around the only Dollar Store on Central Avenue, which had a rather small parking lot. It was quiet and the store had no customers. A few homeless men shuffled by with large bundles of clothes in shopping carts stolen from nearby grocery stores.

Less than an hour later, two big Dodge Ram trucks, pulled into the parking lot. Two men were in each one and they did not enter the store, but remained in their vehicles. Twenty minutes later, the agents observed the green BMW SUV arrive. They watched as two men from one of the trucks get out with a hard-shell blue suitcase on rollers and approach the SUV. The man in the SUV also got out and pulled out a black vinyl athletic bag from the back seat.

Villa, using his radio, gave the order to move in and the loud sound of revved up engines could be heard as several cars began converging on the parking lot. The four gang members, which included Chavez pulled handguns tucked in their waistbands and began to fire. Gunshots rang out causing nearby pedestrians to run in terror across the street. Bullets ricocheted off the asphalt as men tried to hide behind their vehicles. One of the projectiles hit Tanuz in the ankle, but it only caused a minor flesh wound. As the gunfire intensified, Villa saw Chavez running towards the back of the building and gave chase. Chavez turned and fired at Villa, but missed. Villa shot back and two bullets hit the gang leader square in the chest. He fell hard on his back and gasped for air as he drowned in his own blood. He died with his mouth wide open.

Parra and Martinez maneuvered their way around the cars as Quintana, Flores, Gil, and Rodriguez kept the gang members pinned down with a flurry of bullets. Despite being outflanked, the heavily tattooed thugs continued to shoot at the agents. Less than a minute later, all the gang members died with multiple gunshots, including the drug courier. The agents recovered four hundred thousand dollars in cash and twenty kilograms of pure methamphetamine.

In order to preserve the integrity of the ongoing wire

intercept, the DEA had a friendly reporter publish a fictitious story that a couple of DEA agents had stopped at the Dollar Store to buy soft drinks and recognized Chavez who was well known in law enforcement circles. The agents noticed suspicious behavior and then saw an obvious drug exchange and moved in when they were met by a hail of bullets. Other local newspapers and news channels picked up the story.

The money and drug seizures only served to tickle the wire and generate more incriminating conversations. The following day, with rain saturating northern New Mexico, a call came in from Patron to Silva.

Patron stated, "Compadre, I understand you had some problems? Has the situation been contained? I hope what happened doesn't come back to haunt us, understand?"

"No, it was nothing more than bad luck," Silva answered. "Fucking DEA just happened to be at the location by coincidence and saw Chavez there. I don't know why the fuck he had to go, especially since he is so well known. He could have just sent some of his men, but he always wanted to have his finger in the pie and it led to his demise. How are things in Mexico?"

Patron bragged, "We could not be better. Padrino was just promoted and he is now only second to the president of the country. He is protecting our business interests throughout Mexico. Padrino is also getting other high-ranking officials to help us with our enterprise. A week ago, he helped us get some boats to transport some bananas from Colombia, if you know what I mean?"

Silva commented, "That is really great news. Just so you know, I will be sending you a payment in the next two days. Let's talk soon!"

The DEA found the conversation very intriguing and Villa decided to have a meeting with Parra, Tanuz, Martinez, Quintana, Rodriguez, Bert Flores, and Migel Flores. He also invited Alvan Romero and Glenn Holmes from the Criminal Investigation Division of the IRS and Davey Aguilera from the ATF to join them. They were always great additions on collaborative operations and provided added value.

Villa remarked, "Thank you all for attending! We intercepted a conversation between two top ranking Azteca Cartel leaders, one who operates here in New Mexico. In their short discussion, Patron who is based in Mexico stated someone who is apparently a very powerful person is protecting the cartel, second only to the president himself. This is very disturbing news. I have done some research and have determined the secretary of defense is potentially that person since he is directly under the head of state. The current Mexican president, not long ago, promoted General Salvador Cantu to that position."

Martinez stated, "Wow, that puts corruption squarely into the upper echelons of the Mexican government. We have always known it is endemic, but this is mind blowing."

Romero chimed in, "Has any evidence been uncovered of money laundering thus far in the investigation?"

Parra replied, "Not yet, but it is inevitable because they have to be laundering huge amounts of cash."

Villa commented, "We want to bring in the IRS and ATF sooner than later. It would be a great start to begin looking at Silva's finances. I am sure you will uncover a lot of evidence and the techniques he is using to clean the cartel's money."

Romero answered, "Glenn and I will pull his tax records and begin tracing his assets. It will be interesting to determine if he is even a citizen. We will get on it immediately."

A week later, another conversation was intercepted between Silva and Patron. Their discussion revealed a close working relationship with each other and both liked to gossip.

Patron greeted Silva, "Compadre, how are you? We are busy on our end and are getting ready to receive a shipment of toys from China. We will modify them to make them more profitable. I know you know what I mean."

"I know exactly what you mean, Compadre," Silva replied. "It will be great and hopefully; you can send me some soon. I can easily sell them in no time."

Patron stated, "By the way, Padrino called me the other day and he wants to go visit Santa Fe. I hope you don't mind, but I told him that he can stay with you. It would be a good thing for you to show him around."

Silva responded, "Of course! I can take him to different

areas, but he will fall in love with Santa Fe, Espanola, Taos, Albuquerque and other locations. He can do a lot of shopping for some very unusual things."

Patron continued, "Also, we are sending you some really nice shoes. A total of five blue ones. Pedro will take them to Santa Fe and you can meet him at the mall. The usual place. He has a new truck with a double cab. It is rust colored, and has Jalisco plates. He plans to cross into El Paso this Thursday and then head north to your area. Just be ready."

Villa and his men were more than pleased with what the wire was producing, especially with Padrino planning to visit Silva in Santa Fe. For now, they had to deal with the individual coming from Jalisco.

Rapidly, the DEA met with Lieutenants Chris Valdez and Dominic Casados to plan the operation. They would play a critical role and also help separate it from the wire intercept so it would not be disclosed in any judicial proceeding. It was crucial that it continue given the valuable information being obtained. Under the game plan, New Mexico State Police units would be placed on alert for the truck with the Jalisco plates. Valdez and Casados would also be in the Las Cruces area to monitor the situation. Everything was set.

Thursday afternoon, traffic going through Interstate 25 was rather light since most people were at the Pan American Center watching the basketball game between long-time rivals, the Aggies and the Lobos. Valdez and Casados were parked in a marked unit near the New Mexico State University campus when they observed a truck matching the description provided by the DEA. They started to follow and quickly noticed that it had a Jalisco tag. It was going fifteen miles below the speed limit. Everyone in the state normally drove twenty miles above the legal limit.

After about four miles, the two officers turned on their emergency lights, which caused the truck to dramatically increase its speed and take evasive measures by swerving across traffic lanes. Soon, the chase exceeded a hundred miles an hour. Just north of Las Cruces, the speeding truck tried to turn sharply onto a dirt road, but lost control and rolled over three times causing the doors to pop open. The driver, not wearing a seatbelt, fell out and the truck ended up crushing him.

The mangled truck was towed to Albuquerque where the DEA and state police officers tore it apart using drills, hammers, and chisels. They found several secret compartments stuffed with black plastic bags filled with blue fentanyl pills. The total amount was five million with a street value of over thirty million dollars. It was a record haul. Again, the DEA had their reporter friend write an article indicating the man driving the truck had been speeding and was killed while trying to escape from the police.

The very next day, the wire intercept began to heat up

with telephone calls. Things were going badly for the Azteca Cartel in New Mexico and it was not looking well for Silva.

Patron called Silva and stated, "Compadre, what the fuck is going on? We are losing big loads in your state. I am going to pass the phone to Samuel who is here with me."

Samuel came on the line, "Daniel, what is causing the seizure of our merchandise in New Mexico, especially with what happened yesterday!"

Daniel gulped hard and responded, "It is just bad luck and stupid mistakes, but not on my part. I hope you understand?"

"The entire organization has to be more careful, otherwise we will have to start making some examples of people who are careless," Samuel commented. "You can make it up by ensuring Padrino has a good time when he comes to visit New Mexico. He has served us well and you need to make him feel appreciated. Buy him whatever he wants. Everything is on us. Understand?"

"Not to worry, I will treat him like royalty," stated Silva. "Tell Padrino it would be best if he flies into Albuquerque. I can pick him up there. Please let me know a few days in advance that he is coming."

"I will and stay safe," Samuel replied. "Let us know if there is anything we can do on our end to make things go smoother for you, understand?"

Silva felt a sense of relief and responded, "Gracias, I

certainly will and I look forward to meeting Padrino in person very soon."

Villa had Tanuz and Parra conduct a surveillance of Silva's house in Santa Fe before the wire intercept was even initiated. His house was a sprawling adobe structure with a large swimming pool in the back. It was on the road to the local ski basin. Records obtained by Romero showed he paid seven million dollars in cash for it. He lived alone, but always had different women visit him on a regular basis. The house was rather isolated and the area around it was heavily wooded. He had chosen it for a reason. Silva did not have to concern himself with nosy neighbors or prying eyes. Ironically, he had not installed a camera security system in his opulent residence because he was paranoid and believed it could be used against him. The agents knew this because Silva had mentioned in one of his conversations with Patron.

Villa and his men began working with U.S. Attorney Montoya on an affidavit to surreptitiously place listening devices and cameras inside Silva's residence. Once it was completed, the document was presented to U.S. District Judge John Solano. After a careful review, he signed it and the agents went to work. Tanuz, Parra, Quintana, Bert and Migel Flores, Martinez, Rodriguez, and Gil began an intense surveillance of Silva's residence.

The following day, with strong gusty winds sweeping across the dry terrain, Silva drove out alone from his home in his pricey, black Mercedes Maybach GLS. Parra, Martinez, and Quintana followed him in separate cars. The rest remained behind. Once he was observed getting on U.S. 285 heading north, the other agents exited their cars with several black vinyl bags and approached the house. They rang the doorbell. No answer. They quickly picked the door lock and entered. The home was decorated with expensive oil paintings, Persian rugs, and imported furniture. They immediately began their tedious work installing the listening devices and cameras. The plan was to place them in the dining room, kitchen, and living room, areas where most conversations took place. The installation would take several hours. The agents following Silva kept giving the agents at his residence regular updates on his location. They soon reported that he had just passed Española and was headed to Taos on N.M. State Road 68.

The agents at the house drilled holes in the walls and placed micro-camera systems. The listening devices were put in strategic locations. Both the video and audio would be transmitted to the DEA office in Albuquerque where they would be recorded for evidentiary purposes.

The agents tailing Silva watched him visit eight different upscale art galleries in Taos, but he did not stay very long at any of them. Parra jotted down the names and addresses of the galleries on a note pad. They could prove to be of value later on. In the afternoon, Silva began to head south and the agents notified those still in the house that he was on his way back. When Silva was twenty minutes away, the agents finished all their hook-ups, but now had to clean up the residue left by the drilling. They also put everything in its proper place. A single mistake could prove costly. Silva had just entered Santa Fe as the agents locked the front door and jogged back to their cars with only minutes to spare.

Forty-eight hours later, a call the DEA was waiting for came in. It was Patron with exciting news.

Patron spoke loudly, "Compadre, just to inform you that Padrino will be arriving in Albuquerque day after tomorrow at 3:45 p.m. on American Airlines flight 3421 from Mexico City. Make sure your house is immaculate since he is a germaphobe."

"Not to worry, I will be there," Silva answered. "My house is clean and I will take good care of him. Call if you need anything."

Two days later, the DEA agents, IRS agents, Romero and Holmes, and ATF agent Davey Aguilera drove to the airport and were able to observe the arrival of Silva as he entered the terminal. He was alone and wore jeans and eel skin boots. His brown hair was disheveled. He sat on a wooden bench near the tourist shops with his legs crossed and waited.

Thirty minutes passed and the arrival of the American Airlines flight from Mexico City was announced on the airport intercom system. All of the agents went into full alert. Villa, Aguilera, Romero, and Holmes had badged their way through security and stood at the gate where the passengers would disembark. Men, women, and children holding stuffed animals poured out into terminal B. The agents immediately recognized General Cantu, the Mexican Secretary of Defense, from recent photographs, when he stepped out. He was dressed in civilian clothes and had a medium sized suitcase on rollers. He walked purposely until Silva waved at him. General Cantu smiled and shook Silva's hand. They turned and headed out of the terminal. They chatted as they walked to the multilevel parking lot. Agents followed discretely as Silva and Cantu started heading north on I-25 towards Santa Fe. In a little more than an hour, they arrived at Silva's home.

Shortly thereafter, one of the camera's showed them sitting at the kitchen table drinking wine from large goblets. Fortunately, the cameras were functioning very well. The listening devices also picked up crystal clear conversations.

Cantu stated, "Thank you for opening your beautiful home to me. I have always wanted to visit New Mexico, especially Santa Fe. This state belonged to Mexico until the fucking gringos stole it from us. Pinches putos!"

"Yes, they are putos and a bunch of immoral crooks," Silva replied. "I am told you are doing many great things for us and we are very grateful."

Cantu commented, "As long as I am in power all of you can sleep in peace. It is a relationship, which is mutually beneficial. Recently, I was able to get your people some boats to bring in several tons of cocaine from Colombia. I also protected the load until it crossed into this country. It is easy to do these things, especially when you control the entire army."

Silva was heard laughing, then commented, "With you protecting us, our power will be unstoppable. Already, we are the most dominant cartel in the entire world."

Cantu spoke, "The more money the better. I want to have the life of a super wealthy man. The salary paid to me by the government is shit and my pension will only allow me to eat tacos for the rest of my life. I'll take my chances with helping you."

The conversation then shifted to New Mexico, its history and culture, for several hours until they went to bed. When all the lights in the house went out, the agents broke off the surveillance and returned to Albuquerque to get some rest. They would return very early the following day.

The sun was just beginning to rise the next morning and thick, white clouds drifted swiftly across the sky when Quintana, Rodriguez, Gil, and Migel Flores arrived at Silva's house and parked nearby. There were no lights on in the house. The sat in their cars sipping hot coffee and eating crusty croissants they had picked up along the way. Suddenly, several lights went on in front of the residence. Meantime, in the wire intercept room in Albuquerque, Bert Flores, Martinez, Tanuz and Parra listened to the conversations of Cantu and Silva.

Through the well-placed cameras, they could see both men were sitting at the kitchen table drinking coffee.

Silva could be heard saying, "General Cantu, would you like to visit Santa Fe today? You will enjoy the plaza and some other areas."

"Yes, I would very much enjoy that," replied Cantu. "Have you heard anything from your people in Mexico? Three tons of cocaine were coming from Colombia and I had one of my generals in Veracruz providing security."

Silva chuckled loudly, "I have not, but no news is good news. If you are on top of it, I am sure there won't not be any problems."

Cantu laughed and said, "Two weeks ago, the state police in Nayarit discovered one of your methamphetamine labs. I sent some of my men and they chased the police away telling them it was a military project dealing with biological weapons. I had a good laugh that day."

"That is really funny," Silva answered. "Well, let's get ready to leave. There is a lot for you to see."

The agents conducting surveillance saw Silva's black Mercedes roll out into the street and head into the downtown area of Santa Fe. Silva drove into the public parking lot across from the historic Lensic Theater. Silva and Cantu walked towards the plaza. The two suspects entered one jewelry store after the other where Cantu picked out expensive pieces. Silva was seen paying for it all with a credit card.

The two men then strode over to the Cathedral Basilica of Saint Francis of Assisi. Cantu, using his cell phone camera, took pictures of the statue of St. Francis located in front and of the picturesque building with its round arches separated by Corinthian columns and truncated towers. From there they walked a few blocks to the Loretto Chapel. The Sisters of Loretto had commissioned its construction in 1873 for their girl's school. Cantu and Silva stared at its impressive spires, buttresses and stained-glass windows imported from France. Walking into the chapel, Cantu saw the miraculous spiral staircase he had read so much about. It was made mostly of wood and held together with wooden pegs and glue. Amazingly, it was perfectly balanced and stood on its own without any support.

After spending over an hour at the chapel, they walked slowly to one of the diners on the plaza and sat outside near the park. Cantu pointed to a man known as "Doc Santa Fe" who was clad in fur pelts and a wide brimmed hat. He had a long scraggly beard. He looked like an old mountain man. He was a famous fixture in Santa Fe and spent most of his days sitting on a park bench and watching people walk by. Cantu stared at him and one could tell he was very intrigued.

Later that afternoon, they toured the old governor's mansion and visited some of the art galleries. When they walked back to their car, the agents were relieved since most of them were worn out. Within fifteen minutes, Silva drove up to his house and both men went in without a care in the world. The camera in the living room showed them sitting on plush leather sofas. Agents Parra, Martinez, Bert Flores, and Tanuz began to listen intently to the conversation.

Silva remarked, "General Cantu, I hope you enjoyed the day. Now, you can truly understand why the state is called the Land of Enchantment."

"Yes, it one of the most beautiful states I have visited," Cantu replied. "Even better was the quarter of a million dollars you spent on jewelry for me and my family. Thank you! It was a great time to say the least."

The next day, Silva and Cantu visited Espanola and Taos. They stopped at the El Santuario de Chimayo, a historical site, which had an annual pilgrimage of three hundred thousand people. From there, they went to the stunning fifty-mile-long Rio Grande Gorge near Taos. They also visited the nearby Indian pueblo and bought a few trinkets. General Cantu was constantly taking photographs. Just before they started heading back to Santa Fe, the agents watched Cantu quickly take his cell phone out of his pocket and talk for several minutes with a very serious look on his face.

Once they arrived at Silva's house both men were captured by the cameras to be sitting at the kitchen table. They begin sipping wine and General Cantu grabbed a pear from a large fruit bowl and began devouring it.

Silva prodded Cantu, "Please tell me more about your

conversation with one of your commanders. That is very concerning."

Cantu responded, "My subordinate said that the other day, he spoke to a friend who works with the office of the military attaché at the U.S. Embassy in Mexico City and was told the DEA is investigating me for my involvement with your cartel. They must have a snitch who is giving them information. Unfortunately, this means I must change my flight and return home tomorrow. I am not going to take any chances by remaining any longer in this country. I could be arrested at any time."

Silva replied, "I don't blame you. The DEA will not rest until they put you behind bars and they have a worldwide reach."

"I realize that, but as long as I am in Mexico, they cannot touch me despite the bilateral extradition treaty," Cantu commented. "I have too many powerful friends who will protect me, including the president."

Based on the intercepted conversation, Villa and his agents quickly prepared a criminal complaint for Cantu with just enough probable cause in order to buy some more time by avoiding disclosing the wiretap, camera's and listening devices at Silva's residence. They would not arrest Silva, at least not for now. It would allow the DEA along with Romero and Holmes from the IRS to continue their financial investigation into Silva and the Azteca Cartel. U.S Attorney Montoya was notified as was the U.S. Department of Justice and U.S. Department of State because it would be a high-profile arrest, which would have political ramifications. The charge on the complaint was listed as conspiracy to distribute illegal drugs. The magistrate judge approved the complaint and issued an arrest warrant. The agents would have to move fast once Cantu was arrested because under a criminal complaint, the general would be entitled to a preliminary hearing within fourteen days. His defense attorneys would have the right to cross-examine witnesses, which would undoubtedly reveal the existence of the wire intercept.

The next day, storm clouds began to thicken over the skies in northern New Mexico. Agents had been waiting for hours in their cars for Silva and Cantu to head to Albuquerque. They were beginning to get anxious when suddenly Silva's car appeared and came out onto the road. They followed at a distance. As expected, the two suspects took I-25 and headed south.

In less than an hour, the car driven by Silva pulled up to the departure area of the Albuquerque International Airport and it was now starting to rain. Cantu jumped out the car and ran into the building pulling his suitcase. Villa and his agents waited until Silva was several miles away before moving in and arresting the general. He was shocked.

Cantu protested and said, "How can you arrest me? I am

the Secretary of Defense for Mexico. You are making a big mistake and will pay dearly for your transgression."

Villa looked at him and stated, "By the time you get out of prison, Mexico will have had over three different Secretaries of Defense. You are done!"

Cantu was read his rights in Spanish and nodded he understood them. He was quickly taken to one of the federal magistrates for initial presentment. At the hearing, the charges against him were read and then he was given to the custody of the U.S. Marshals. He was put in a tiny prison cell where his anxiety levels skyrocketed.

The media throughout the world covered the story of Cantu's arrest the following day. They only knew of the charges, but were unaware they stemmed from an ongoing wiretap. The Azteca Cartel, including Silva, believed the DEA had an informant who had betrayed Cantu. The DEA and IRS now had to move quickly and efficiently.

With the collaborative efforts of Romero and Holmes, they discovered that the cartel was laundering money through art galleries in Taos and Santa Fe. Tens of millions of dollars flowed regularly through these businesses, despite almost never selling any works of art. It was a total façade. They also located several accounts at local banks under Silva's true identity. He had stupidly opened the accounts in his name believing they could be explained away using the galleries as cover. He was mistaken. The bank accounts totaled two hundred million dollars and they were all seized. Days later, a search warrant was executed at Silva's house. In the garage, they found a large, heavy safe, which was drilled open. Ten million dollars in bundles of hundred-dollar bills were found and confiscated. In the basement, the agents found numerous huge plastic bins full of cocaine, methamphetamine, fentanyl, and heroin totaling a whopping two tons. Four crates of AR-15s were also located and ATF agent Aguilera took custody of them. He would conduct traces on them through his agency's data base, E-Trace. Silva was taken into custody as he yelled obscenities at the top of his lungs.

Alarico and Samuel were dismayed when they heard the news of General Cantu and Silva. As cartel leaders, setbacks were to be expected and they had built the Azteca Cartel to be resilient by compartmentalizing their operations. If someone was arrested and decided to cooperate, they would only be able to provide limited information to law enforcement. Money allowed them to replace anybody or anything for that matter.

The extremely successful operation in New Mexico was definitely a big punch to the gut of the Azteca Cartel, but Villa knew they would bounce back. Much work still needed to be done.

The Mexican president through his foreign minister pressured the U.S. to return Cantu back to their country with the assurance they would prosecute him there. Even a blind man could see that it would never happen. Cantu and Silva were given life sentences plus thirty years. Unfortunately, Cantu dodged his prison sentence by dying two years later from a heart attack.

CHAPTER 12

THE WITNESS

It was uncomfortably hot and humid. The sound of rushing waves from the Pacific Ocean slammed loudly against the sandy shore. Alarico and Samuel were in Puerto Vallarta, Jalisco, sipping frozen margaritas with Albanian gangster Agron Shehu who had come to Mexico to meet with the cartel leaders. Shehu controlled a transnational criminal organization based in Belgium. He was tall, muscular and his good looks were rather disarming. He was born in the rugged mountain hamlet of Theth, Albania, whose sun kissed peaks towered over the wooden patches of the area. When Shehu was a teenager, two men got into a fight with his father over local politics and ended up shooting him in the face with a shotgun. Much to the dismay of his family, he had to have a closed coffin funeral service. It sent shockwaves through his poor family and revenge consumed Shehu for weeks.

One night, he followed one of the men who had killed his father as he left his house. When he turned the corner onto a quiet street, Shehu pounced like a ravenous lion. He repeatedly stabbed the man with a sharp butcher knife. Then he began to slice through tissue and cervical discs until he fully decapitated him. Like a piece of trash, he threw his head towards a pack of wild dogs that began devouring it.

It was a dark night and the cold mountain air swept down on Theth. It was quiet and everyone was in bed trying to stay warm. A shadowy figure walked with a purposeful stride toward the house of his target. It was Shehu. He popped open a window in front of the small, quaint house and quietly slithered inside like a serpent. Silently, he crept to the sole bedroom and found the door ajar. With deep hatred, Shehu looked momentarily at his father's other killer. He took a large gourd full of gasoline, which he had brought with him and began to douse the sleeping man with it. The wetness awoke him and he groggily looked up at Shehu. Before he could utter a word, the man saw a lit match drop from Shehu's right hand. A second later, his bed burst into flames. His flesh began to blister and his lungs burned as he inhaled the intense heat. He screamed and leaped from the bed and right into the knife of Shehu, which was plunged deep into his heart.

The very next day, Shehu fled Albania after saying goodbye to his mother. He decided to go to Brussels, Belgium, where he had some close friends. To support himself, he took a job as a waiter at the Restaurant Le Rabassier. A year later, he decided to enroll at the prestigious Univerité Libre de

Bruxelles where he majored in foreign languages. Apart from Albanian, he learned French, Dutch, German, and Spanish fluently.

After graduating from college, he met a man from Amsterdam at a local bar and in conversation Shehu learned he was a trafficker of MDMA, better known as ecstasy. It was a drug that increased energy, empathy, and pleasure. It was Shehu's entry into drug trafficking.

Later, he began selling cocaine, but was ripped off by Colombian suppliers to the tune of a million dollars. He had advanced them the money and they never delivered the merchandise. In desperation, Shehu reached out to a Mexican acquaintance he had befriended in college who managed to put him in contact with Alarico. And now, here he was in the company of the most feared drug lord in the world.

Alarico commented, "You must be determined for you to travel all the way from Europe to do business with us. What is it that we can help you with?"

Shehu replied, "The demand for cocaine is growing very rapidly throughout the European continent and it has become more profitable than ever. I want to be a part of that lucrative business."

"Won't it be better for you to buy it directly from the Colombians?" asked Samuel. "I am sure you could find a source and it would be even cheaper for you."

With a look of dismay, Shehu stated, "I have had very bad

luck dealing directly with the Colombians. I would rather deal with you even if I have to pay more. I have been told by many people of your solid reputations."

Alarico smiled and stated, "We are drug traffickers, not crooks. What type of quantities are we talking about and will you require us to transport the cocaine to you? If that is the case, the price will increase to cover those costs."

"For the foreseeable future, you will need to handle transportation. My organization, at the present time, does not have that type of capability," replied Shehu. "I will purchase ton quantities from you depending on the price."

"Since you obviously know the price from Colombian wholesalers is three thousand dollars a kilo, we will let you have them for five thousand, which will include transportation," stated Samuel. "We guarantee all of our shipments and you have our word on that."

Alarico asked, "Where do you want us to transport the cocaine? I assume somewhere in Europe?"

Shehu responded, "The cocaine has to be delivered to the Belgium port of Antwerp. I have many contacts there and the location is a more central location in Europe than most of the North Sea ports. Another big advantage is the docks there are connected to the hinterland by rail, road, river, and canal waterways. It is a virtual smuggler's paradise."

Alarico became pensive and stated, "Samuel, I have an idea. We can ship the cocaine from Colombia into Costa

Rica with relative ease. Shipments of cargo from a country that does not produce drugs undergo less scrutiny by customs officials. We have, on occasion, used Puerto Limon in that country to ship to different locations around the world. It has three large terminals and Costa Rica recently upgraded the entire port making shipments from there much easier."

Shehu asked, "Where in Costa Rica is this port located? Moving drugs long distance is a very complicated task!"

"The port is situated on the Caribbean side of Costa Rica," replied Alarico. "We can put the cocaine in maritime containers and conceal it under several tons of bananas. We have a contact who owns several maritime ships and transports cargo to Europe on a regular basis. He will help us, for or a fee, of course."

Alarico took out his cell phone and used the calculator application to determine how long it would take for cargo to reach Antwerp from Costa Rica. He knew that Antwerp was about nine thousand kilometers from Puerto Limon and if the maritime ship traveled at twenty-five knots (forty-six kilometers per hour) it would take about eight days to reach Belgium. It was longer than airfreight, but would be much more secure.

"Shehu, once we ship the cocaine from Puerto Limon, you will have it in approximately eight days and Samuel will ensure close coordination to keep you apprised of its movement to your area," stated Alarico. "Also, you will pay us by wire transferring the necessary amounts to bank accounts we have here in Mexico. We have several large businesses in the country to make the money appear legitimate. Are we in agreement?"

Shehu smiled and responded, "We definitely have a deal. I guarantee you we will make a ton of money working together. Now let's drink to good fortune."

Alarico, Samuel, and Shehu drank late into the night and finally staggered to their hotel rooms. All three fell into an alcohol induced deep sleep. The next morning, Alarico had two of his men drive Shehu to Guadalajara where he caught a direct Air France flight to Brussels. Alarico and Samuel remained in Puerto Vallarta for a couple more days. Their cartel had grown so much they seldom had any time for enjoyment. They worked with criminals, but did not entirely trust them. The cartel leaders knew everyone under them would take advantage of any opportunity to seize control of the Azteca Cartel. Their guard was always up. Any mistake could have severe consequences.

Two weeks later, Samuel arrived at the Juan Santamaria International Airport located in the city of Alajuela, Costa Rica, which was a twenty-minute drive to the capital of San Jose. He was met by Jose Agapito Candelaria, an Azteca Cartel operative, who oversaw the smuggling of cocaine from Colombia through Central America. Candelaria was built like a fire hydrant and had been involved in crime from early childhood. It was rumored he had killed dozens of men, some just for the pleasure of it. He was appropriately nicknamed "the assassin." Candelaria had been born in Los Ojos, in northern New Mexico and had been recruited by Silva into the cartel. The two men exited the airport and walked into a rustic parking lot where Candelaria had parked his immaculate, black Toyota Land Cruiser.

In minutes, both men were on their way to Puerto Limon. They drove through the busy streets of San Jose then got on Route 32. Traffic soon ran into a minor problem as heavy rainfall had caused a landslide blocking the road. Dozens of men with shovels worked furiously to clear the small mountain of dirt. After an hour, a member of the road crew waved them through. After five hours, Samuel and Candelaria finally arrived at Puerto Limon and immediately went to Palomino Transportes Maritimos, which was the largest maritime shipping company in the country. Both men were escorted to the office of the owner, Vicente Palomino who was of medium build and had hazel eyes and brown hair. He was a no-nonsense man who had built his company from scratch and sheer bribery. He stood up and shook hands with both men.

Palomino stated, "Samuel, it has been at least a year since I have seen you. Normally, you send your men to deal with me, so I guess it must be important for you to come all this way?"

Samuel replied, "It is important. We have a new customer

in Brussels, Belgium, and we will be shipping him tons of cocaine on a regular basis. In order to accomplish this, we need your transportation services. We will bring the cocaine from Cartagena, Colombia, on fishing boats and then the rest is up to you. You will be paid the usual fee of three hundred dollars for each kilo you transport. Do you agree?"

"I totally understand and accept the deal," Palomino replied. "It is no risk to me because if the cocaine was discovered, I would be in the clear since it is not my job to search the containers. That falls on the port authority and I can bribe them for less than five thousand dollars a load. It is a win, win situation for everyone."

Candelaria commented, "I will be in charge of coordinating the transport of cocaine with you and the Colombians. Once it is on its way to Antwerp, I will coordinate with the people there. As long as everyone carries out their responsibilities there should be no problems."

"That is correct, Jose will handle all of the logistics and coordination," Samuel stated. "We plan on sending the first load of two tons next week. The amounts will undoubtedly increase as we move forward. Well, I guess this concludes our business unless you have any questions."

Smiling, Palomino responded, "No, it is quite simple for me. All I have to do is load the cocaine into one of my boats and point it in the right direction. That is simpler than having a civil conversation with my wife."

Everyone laughed at the comment. Samuel and Candelaria left and drove to San Jose and checked into the five-star, Springs Resort and Spa Hotel. It had an amazing view of the Arenal Volcano. The rooms, with wooden floors, were extremely spacious and beautifully decorated. Later, they went to the hot springs and soaked for an hour and then had the famed, blackened, red snapper for dinner at the hotel restaurant. Afterwards, they had a few drinks of guaro mixed with Coca Cola. Guaro was the national drink of the country and was made from fermented sugar cane known as aguardiente (water that burns). Both men were tired so they went to their rooms and made it an early night.

Early the next day, Candelaria drove Samuel to the airport. Samuel returned to Guadalajara pleased with the way things had gone in Puerto Limon and conveyed all of the details to Alarico who was elated with the news.

Six days later, with the moon reflecting off the swirling waters of the Caribbean, a large fishing boat, made of fiberglass, approached the coastline of Tortuguero. It was Costa Rica's version of the Amazon rainforest. The area was a series of rivers and canals that crisscrossed the jungle. Drug smugglers used it for their criminal activities. Another distinct advantage was everyone preferred living at or visiting the Pacific side of the country. The infrastructure and accommodations on the Caribbean side were not as good. For drug smugglers it was more than great.

The fishing boat got very close to the shore and flashed its powerful lights three times. Candelaria quickly ordered eight large canoes into the water. It took a several minutes for them to come alongside the fishing boat. Men rapidly begin passing twenty-kilogram bales of cocaine down to the smaller boats. As each canoe was loaded, it made its way back to shore where other men formed a line and passed the bales quickly to one another until they were loaded onto a tractor-trailer. The entire operation took less than an hour. Within forty-five minutes, the loaded truck arrived at Puerto Limon. Under the cover of darkness, the men entered the port and quickly took the bales of cocaine from the truck and loaded them into a maritime container at Palomino's business. Hundreds of boxes of unripe bananas were carefully placed over them.

The following day, a gigantic port crane lifted the forty-foot container with the cocaine and hoisted it onto a huge container ship. By late afternoon, as the sun was setting, the ship left the port and began to slice its way through the blue Caribbean waters. Candelaria then called Shehu.

"I just wanted to let you know that your elderly grandmother has left and is heading home," Candelaria advised. "Let me know when she arrives so we are without worry."

Shehu replied, "That is really great news. I look forward to seeing my beloved grandmother. It has been quite some time. I will let you know the minute she arrives. Thanks for calling."

In eight and a half days, the cocaine arrived in Antwerp and members of Shehu's organization were there waiting. Belgium officials opened the container and just slightly glanced in and signed the documentation clearing the shipment. They had been paid off. Within days, the cocaine was broken up into smaller amounts and sent to Germany, France, Italy, Spain, United Kingdom, Greece, and the Czech Republic. Some of it was distributed to the addict population in Belgium.

Three weeks passed and Candelaria, based on conversations with Shehu, sent another five tons of cocaine to him. Hundreds of millions of dollars were pouring into bank accounts in Mexico controlled by Alarico and the Azteca Cartel.

One stormy afternoon, despite local weather forecasters predicting sunny skies, Villa was in his office when he received a call from a man who refused to identify himself. Villa could tell he was nervous by his quavering voice. The man stated he had information on two individuals who had been buying hundreds of AR-15s and stockpiling them in a house in Lordsburg, New Mexico. He identified the two men as Apolonio and Ramiro Apodaca who were brothers. He added they worked for the Azteca Cartel and had been buying large quantities of weapons for them. Apparently, in the past several years they had shipped thousands, which had been used to kill an untold number of people. He described it as a river of iron flowing into Mexico. The weapons were purchased on the internet and large gun shows, which effectively circumvented background checks. The man told Villa the stash of weapons they currently had would soon be smuggled into Mexico. He also provided the address where the two brothers lived. Before hanging up, Villa gave the man his cell number in the event he came up with additional information.

The following morning, Villa had a meeting with agents Chris Quintana, Migel Flores, Emmanuel Rodriquez, David Gil, Lupe Martinez, Mike Parra, Ed Tanuz and Bert Flores. Also, present were IRS agents Alvan Romero, Glenn Holmes, and Davey Aguilera from the ATF.

Villa stated, "Yesterday, I received a call from a man who was scared to death. He provided information on two brothers, Apolonio and Ramiro Apodaca who apparently have been buying a lot of assault rifles for the Azteca Cartel. He gave me their address in Lordsburg and apparently they are going to smuggle a lot of AR-15s into Mexico soon. I ran the names of the Apodaca brothers through our database and both are suspected cocaine and heroin traffickers. We are all going to Lordsburg and establish a surveillance on their house. Right now, we don't have sufficient probable cause for a search warrant, but maybe we will be able to establish it by watching their movements.

Late that evening, the agents arrived in Lordsburg, which was in southern New Mexico. It was located in northern Hidalgo County, at the intersection of U.S. Route 70 and I-10. The population of the county was less than five thousand inhabitants and had an eight-mile border with Mexico. The area was a farming, ranching, and mining community. It was a sleepy town with little law enforcement presence.

Without much trouble, the agents were able to locate the Apodaca residence. It was a white house with a wraparound porch. In the back was an old barn. Two blue Chevrolet Silverado trucks were parked in front. It was eerily quiet with a soft breeze lifting dry leaves into the air. Quintana and Gil would remain on surveillance behind a clump of elm trees. The other agents checked into the nearly vacant Hampton Inn near the center of town.

Very early the next morning, while it was still dark, Villa, Parra, Tanuz, Romero, and Holmes arrived in two cars and took over for Quintana and Gil. Before sunrise, lights went on in the house and movement could be seen inside. Two hours passed, when the agents suddenly saw a mud-covered Dodge Ram truck coming down the road pulling a horse trailer. It slowly turned into the narrow dirt entrance to the house. It parked near the barn and a minute later, a couple of men came out of the house and shook hands with two burly men who exited the truck. Not long after, all four men were seen loading the trailer, not with horses, but with large bales. They certainly didn't appear to be alfalfa.

Immediately, Villa called and had Migel and Bert Flores, Martinez, Aguilera, and Rodriquez establish a position further down the road and standby until further notice. Things were about to get interesting very quickly. Half an hour later, the four men finished their labor and stood chatting for several minutes. They shook hands and the two men who had arrived entered their truck and began to drive away slowly.

Villa got on his radio and contacted the agents down the road, "Please be advised, there is a white truck with a horse trailer heading in your direction. It appears to be loaded with drugs. Stop it and try to get consent to search the trailer. If that fails, have the state police send a drug sniffing dog. If it alerts on it, that is sufficient probable cause to get a search warrant. The rest of us will stay on the Apodaca house. Copy?"

"We copy and we can see the truck approaching our position," Aguilera responded. "It is traveling really slow so it must be hauling a lot of weight."

A very long fifteen minutes passed and finally Aguilera came on the radio, "The trailer is carrying a ton of marijuana and half a ton of cocaine. The two men, who have outstanding arrest warrants out of Colorado for drug distribution, did not initially want to give consent for us to do a search, but changed their mind when we told them a drug detection dog was on its way. Both of them signed the consent to search form. Now they can't deny giving their permission later on."

"Great job, the rest of us are now going to secure the Apodaca house until we can get a search warrant," Villa replied. "We certainly don't want them to destroy any evidence."

With the sound of roaring engines, Villa, and the agents

with him, drove rapidly to the front of the house. As they were getting out of their vehicles, they heard loud blasts from high powered rifles and jumped for cover. They quickly returned fire from behind their vehicles. Gunshots shattered windows and bullets penetrated metal. A bullet from one of the agents hit a large aromatic candle burning in the living room. It flew two meters right into the burgundy, satin curtains of a nearby window, which exploded into flames. In a flash, the entire room was on fire, but the men inside continued to engage the agents in a horrific gun battle. Heavy clouds of gray smoke soon began to billow out of the entire house. It hung over the area like an ominous fog.

Suddenly, the front door swung open and the Apodaca brothers charged out shooting wildly and screaming, "fuck you." The weapons from the agents spit fire and lead killing both men. The house was now a huge fireball.

Despite the intense heat, the agents went to the barn, and stashed between several bales of hay they discovered over three hundred AR-15s in wooden crates and five hundred kilograms of cocaine. The citizens of Lordsburg were shocked to find out that members of the powerful Azteca Cartel were living among them. It created suspicion and paranoia in the small community for months.

One evening, Villa took Parra, Martinez, Tanuz, Romero, Holmes, Aguilera, Quintana, Rodriguez, Gil, Bert and Migel Flores, Chris Valdez, and Dominic Casados out to dinner to celebrate their recent successes against the Azteca Cartel. U.S. Attorney Lillie Montoya joined them. They decided to go to the best restaurant in New Mexico, El Paragua, located in Espanola. The music was loud and the restaurant, as always, was crowded. A song suddenly blared out of the establishments sound system by the famous Mexican singer, Alberto Angel AKA El Cuervo:

"1950, señores. I am going to tell you the story of a very famous man covered in glory, born in Espanola, New Mexico. His father was a great warrior during World War II. He was known for his bravery."

Everyone toasted with a shot of tequila and enjoyed each other's company. There was no greater bond between anyone than that forged by shared danger and putting your life in the hands of others.

The chili was hot and Tanuz commented he was very happy the restaurant didn't put any cumin in it like so many other restaurants in the state. When he went to the restroom, everyone decided to get him a five-pound bag of the spice as a joke. After great merriment, the agents called it a night and drove back to Albuquerque.

Days later, Villa received a call at the office from a woman who identified herself as Theresa Sanchez. Theresa stated she worked at a clinic just south of Albuquerque and one of their patients was gravely ill with COVID-19.

Theresa commented, "Mr. Campos requested you come

right away. He knows he has little time left. He said it would be of great benefit for you to meet with him."

Villa responded, "What is his full name? I would like to check him out in our database."

Villa could hear Theresa talk to someone and then she came back on the line. She was very calm.

"Sorry, I had to get his permission to give you his personal information," Theresa stated, "His name is Matt Campos and he was born on August 12, 1980 in Los Ojos, New Mexico."

Theresa gave Villa the address of the clinic and also her telephone number so he could let her know what time he would be arriving. He informed her he and other agents would be there in less than an hour. Villa quickly ran Campos's name in the DEA indices, which revealed that he was involved in major drug trafficking activities in Mexico and Central America.

In less than twenty minutes, Villa, Parra, Tanuz, and Romero were on the way to the clinic and arrived quickly since there was little traffic on the highway. The clinic was very small and housed in a rectangular structure. Theresa was patiently waiting outside. She had wavy, brown hair and brown eyes. She had a mask on and other protective gear. Theresa told the agents that Campos, after talking with his elderly mother, wanted to confess to his crimes hoping to enter heaven with a cleansed soul. Theresa swiftly handed out medical facemasks, gloves, and gowns to the agents. She then escorted them to a small room where a man was praying and looking up at the ceiling. He was heavy set, with a triple chin, black hair and brown eyes. He coughed loudly as he looked at the agents.

Villa told him, "Mr. Campos, we are from the DEA and IRS. We understand you want to speak with us. We are sorry about your condition."

Campos, with extremely labored breathing, replied, "Thank you! And thank you for coming. My time on this earth is limited, and I promised my mother I would do an act of contrition by confessing to my criminal acts. I was born in Los Ojos in the northern part of the state. My friend from childhood, Jose Agapito Candelaria, is a high-ranking Azteca Cartel leader responsible for operations in Central America. He is the one who brought me into a life of crime. I worked with Candelaria and others in transporting tons of cocaine from Colombia into Mexico and ultimately into the U.S. The cartel is now moving a huge amount into Europe, especially Belgium. They are working with the violent Albanian Mafia and the boss is a man named Agron Shehu."

Villa asked, "Is the cocaine going directly to Belgium from Colombia? Also, where can Candelaria be located?"

Campos, coughing loudly, stated, "The cocaine is being smuggled from Colombia into Costa Rica, on a regular basis, using fishing boats. It is then put on maritime container ships and transported by a company called Palomino Transportes

Maritimos in Puerto Limon. The owner, Vicente Palomino, is in cahoots with the cartel. From Costa Rico, it goes to the Belgium port of Antwerp. Eventually, it is distributed throughout Europe. Candelaria is currently staying in San Jose, Costa Rica. He is the one handling all of the drug shipments through that country. Please get my wallet from the nightstand drawer and in it is a small piece of paper with his name and cell telephone number on it."

Parra retrieved the wallet and quickly found it. It was frayed with water stains, but the name and number were still legible.

"Do you happen to know the address where Candelaria is staying in Costa Rica?" Tanuz asked. "Does he live alone and when is the last time you saw him?"

Campos strained to reply, "He has been staying in room 401 at the Grand Hotel Costa Rica, which is one of the better hotels in the city. He has set up a command-and-control center in his room using HF/VHF/UHF radio frequencies for communications. Because of his large tips, the hotel staff ignores the obvious, and they just go along with it. He stays by himself and works most of the day."

Romero inquired, "How do the Albanians pay the Azteca Cartel and what does the cartel do with the money once they receive it?"

Campos was tiring quickly, but replied, "The cartel has many businesses that include dairy farms, shopping malls, movie theaters, clothing boutiques, farm equipment, and many others. They are laundering billions of dollars each year and therefore are into every business you can imagine. The Albanians are wire transferring the money into cartel bank accounts in Mexico by making it appear they are legitimate transactions."

Before Campos completely faded out, Villa asked Theresa if they could borrow a computer for a few minutes. She quickly took the agents to a vacant office, which had everything they needed, including privacy. It took Parra less than fifteen minutes to type out a confession for Campos to sign based on the information he had provided. Villa knew that dying declarations were an exception to the hearsay rule and would be accepted by U.S. courts, if it was given in good faith and Campos was conscious of his impending death and fully believed there was no hope of recovery.

The agents went back to see Campos and he was read the statement since he was incapable of reading it himself. He stated it was accurate and fortunately he was able to sign it. The agents thanked Theresa profusely for all her assistance and returned to their office. Much work needed to be done.

The following day, Villa had a meeting in the DEA's conference room to discuss a strategy to dismantle the Azteca Cartel based on the information provided by Campos.

Villa commented, "We were very lucky to have spoken with Campos yesterday who provided us with valuable data regarding the Azteca Cartel's operations in Europe and their ties to the Albanian mob. We have to put our minds together and devise a comprehensive strategy in order to destroy the cartel, top to bottom. It will require significant coordination with many international partners and the full exploitation of evidence that will be developed as a result. We will also have to navigate through the landmines of political corruption to ensure our investigation is not compromised."

Romero stated, "It is going to require extraordinary effort on everyone's part to be able to accomplish this huge effort."

"You can count of the ATF, and we will put in whatever time and resources are necessary," Aguilera stated.

"I agree we have to be very careful we don't fuck up the operation by dealing with corrupt security forces in the countries we will be working with," retorted Parra.

I can see we will be doing a lot of travel since there is nothing like face-to-face coordination," acknowledged Holmes.

Villa stated, "Well, the first order of business will be for some of us to travel to Costa Rica and meet with Juan Morales, the head of the Policia de Control de Drogas (Drug Control Police), which is under the Ministry of Public Security. He is a good friend of mine and can be trusted to work with us on this operation. Morales is honest and has been a loyal public servant to his country for many years.

"So, what do you have in mind?" asked Martinez. "This is going to be a huge undertaking!"

Villa smiled, "First, we need to convince the Costa Rican Policia de Control de Drogas to initiate a wire intercept on both Candelaria's and Palomino's phones. Next, we will meet the Belgium Federale Politie (Federal Police) and advise them of the shipments of cocaine being smuggled through Antwerp from Puerto Limon. We will have them start looking into Shehu. We also need to work with the Colombian National Police to identify the sources of supply for the cocaine being sold by the Azteca Cartel. That will be our strategy for now."

Three days later, Villa, Parra, Tanuz, Romero, Holmes, and Martinez were on a flight to Costa Rica. On arrival, they rented a large van and drove to the Public Security Ministry where Morales's office was located. They parked in front of the concrete three-story building with bright blue and orange trim. A uniformed police officer escorted the group of American agents to the third floor where Morale's office was located. Morales, a short, thin man with gleaming white teeth and a mustache stood up from his chair and embraced Villa.

Morales stated, "Miguel, it is so good to see you! I have not seen you since the International Drug Enforcement Conference in Bolivia. Who are these men with you?"

"It is great seeing you as well," Villa replied. "This is Ed Tanuz, Mike Parra, Alvan Romero, Glenn Holmes, and Lupe Martinez. All of them work with me."

"So, what brings you to Costa Rica?" Morales asked. "Let me guess, you have a major operation involving my country, right?"

Villa laughed and responded, "How did you know? We have received information that the Mexican Azteca Cartel is shipping tons of cocaine from Puerto Limon to Antwerp, Belgium. The coordinator for those shipments is a man named Jose Agapito Candelaria who is apparently staying in room 401 at the Grand Hotel Costa Rica. He is working with Vicente Palomino who owns Palomino Transportes Maritimos. Here is Candelaria's cell number. I wrote it down for you. We want to work this investigation with you. It is absolutely critical Candelaria's cell phone and the telephone in his room be intercepted as soon as possible. It is also important to intercept Palomino's office, home, and cell phones as well. We don't have those, but I am sure you can obtain them discretely from your contacts at the telephone company. Let's not do physical surveillance on them for now. We don't want to heat up the situation and make them more cautious and suspicious."

Morales smiled and stated, "Miguel, you are like a wolf who is more interested in the hunt than on survival. If I were a criminal, I would not want you on my trail. I have never seen anyone more tenacious than you. Not to worry, I will move quickly in intercepting Candelaria's phones and also Palomino's."

Villa asked, "Do you mind if I leave Tanuz, Holmes, and Martinez to work with you here in Costa Rica? I will be traveling to Belgium tomorrow with Romero and Parra to meet with the authorities there. As you know, most of the critical work on international cases involves close coordination."

"I would very much appreciate you leaving some of your men to work with us," Morales stated. "We have our hands full with all the crime we are currently experiencing. Besides, they can keep you apprised of everything we are doing."

"Thank you, my friend," Villa commented. "I can always count on you. Best of luck!"

The following morning, Villa, Romero, and Parra boarded Iberian Flight 2398 to Madrid, Spain and from there they would catch a connecting flight to Brussels. The entire journey would take almost twenty hours. Fortunately, they were able to get first class seats, which would make it more comfortable with the added leg room. To pass the time, all three watched onboard movies and took catnaps.

After the long trip, they finally landed at the Adolfo Suárez Madrid-Barajas Airport. It was the second largest airport in Europe and the terminal was bustling with tourists arriving from countries around the world. The agents had a little over an hour to kill before their flight to Brussels so they went to a little restaurant within the airport. They each ordered patatas bravas, which were small, fried chunks of potatoes with a generous topping of fiery red sauce. Villa's sweet tooth got the best of him and he also ordered churros, which were hot, fried dough in the shape of a long, spiral, covered in sugar. It came with a small, white bowl of melted chocolate. Villa smiled with pleasure.

Subsequent to finishing their meal, Villa and the others walked to the Lufthansa gate and soon boarded the large aircraft. After the door to the aircraft was closed, one of the flight attendants got on the intercom and advised the passengers that the flight to Brussels would be two hours. Villa fell asleep as the plane climbed rapidly into the sky and before he knew it, he felt the plane shudder as its wheels touched down on the runway. Entering the terminal, they walked to a car rental and obtained a black Toyota Camry. The agents were soon on their way to federal police headquarters.

In thirty minutes, they arrived at the modern police building decorated with multi-colored rectangular panels. Once inside, the men were quickly taken to the spacious office of Marc Voss, General Commissioner of the Federal Police. Voss was a tall, slender man with short blond hair and wore a blue suit with a black tie. He greeted the agents and invited them to sit in black leather chairs. Villa had done some research on Voss and knew he spoke English, Dutch, German, and French. He was a highly respected official within the government and was known for his unwavering integrity.

Voss stated, "Gentlemen, I want to welcome you to Belgium. We are very grateful to America for helping liberate our country from German occupation during WWII. Many of your soldiers gave their lives for our country."

"Thank you, my Uncle Ramon was killed during the Battle of the Bulge," replied Villa. "He was a staff sergeant with the 82 Airborne Division and was only twenty-three years old when he died. He is buried at the Henri-Chapelle Cemetery."

Voss commented, "You should take time to visit the cemetery while you are here. It is only seventy miles from Brussels. But back to business, what brings the DEA to Belgium?"

Villa remarked, "We have been conducting an investigation involving a multi-national drug trafficking organization in Mexico called the Azteca Cartel and they are shipping tons of cocaine from Costa Rica to Belgium through Antwerp. The recipient of the drugs is an Albanian gangster by the name of Agron Shehu."

"We are fully aware of Shehu," stated Voss. "He has been implicated in several murders, but he is a slippery character and we have never been able to pin any crimes on him. We have Shehu's cell number and the address where he lives. Unfortunately, we have been totally focused on Islamic terrorist cells operating in our country for the past several years. Last year alone, we conducted over seven thousand wiretaps on terrorists, which was a record for us. In Belgium, wire intercepts are limited to serious crime cases, such as human trafficking or terrorist crime. Fortunately, drug trafficking also falls into that category. Based on the information you have given me; we will be able to get an order from one of our judges to begin tapping Shehu's phone."

Romero mentioned, "We are also very interested on any information you obtain in terms of money laundering activities. We have a keen capability to trace money transactions around the globe."

"Of course," Voss replied. "Let's continue to coordinate this investigation closely. We will do anything to keep illegal drugs off our streets. I will personally keep you informed of anything we develop on our end. Thank you for coming."

Villa, Romero, and Parra decided to visit the Henri-Chapelle Cemetery since their flight was not until the following morning. They arrived in less than an hour and were totally impressed with the beautiful fifty-seven acres where so many American heroes were buried. The white headstones were arranged in gentle arcs sweeping across a broad, green lawn that sloped downhill. They found Villa's uncle Ramon's gravesite in the middle of all the tombstones. He had parachuted behind enemy lines during the Normandy invasion, was wounded, hospitalized and once strong enough he was sent to Belgium. Ramon was killed during the famous Battle of the Bulge. Ramon was the brother of Villa's father, Samuel, who was captured in the Philippines and forced to participate in the infamous Bataan Death March. He was taken to a POW camp in Osaka, Japan, until the end of the war. Both Ramon and Samuel were genuine heroes and served their country with honor and gallantry.

The following morning, the agents spent all day on a very long, tiring flight back to New Mexico. All were exhausted, but were tenacious and driven. They would chase the devil into hell if necessary.

CHAPTER 13

THE TAKEDOWN

The day after Villa, Romero and Parra returned to New Mexico, a call was received from Holmes in San Jose. He sounded very excited.

Holmes commented, "Miguel, we have started picking up some interesting conversations on Candelaria's cell phone. He has been speaking directly with Alvaro Santos, the leader of the Gulf Clan Cartel in Colombia. They have been talking in code, but it was relatively easy to understand they are planning an operation involving ten tons of cocaine. Santos advised that the cocaine, which he calls pottery, would be ready by next week. Candelaria and Palomino have also been communicating several times a day. Palomino told him that he was ready to send one of his ships to Europe, but would wait for Candelaria to deliver his illegal cargo to the port."

"That is very interesting," Villa replied. "I have an idea. We could probably just make the seizure in Costa Rica, but that would not help us take down Shehu and his people. I would like to put a transponder on the Palomino ship, if possible, that will transport the cocaine to Antwerp. Using this tactic, we can let the federal police in Belgium know when it approaches their coast so they can prepare a warm welcome for the Albanian mob. The seizure of the cocaine will be valuable evidence for them to use against Shehu and his associates."

Holmes replied, "That is a great idea. We are getting excellent cooperation from our counterparts here in Costa Rica. We take them out to dinner on a regular basis as a small reward."

"Glad you are doing that since they don't make a lot of money," Villa stated. "A small gesture of kindness goes a long way. Please keep me posted. I will send Parra to San Jose tomorrow with a micro-transponder. He is an expert on their use and can install them very effectively."

"OK, we will pick him up at the airport and also reserve a room for him here at the hotel," responded Holmes. "Looks like fireworks in the near future. Take care!"

The following day, Parra took an afternoon flight to Costa Rica and was picked up at the airport by Holmes, Tanuz, and Martinez. Parra carried the transponder in his suitcase, which had two super powerful magnets on it. Once it was attached to metal it would take a crowbar to pry it loose.

That same day, Villa called his friend, Todd Smith, at the National Reconnaissance Office (NRO) based in Chantilly,

Virginia. The NRO, a member of the intelligence community, which included the CIA, National Security Agency, Defense Intelligence Agency, and National Geospatial-Intelligence Agency. The NRO reported to National Intelligence and the Secretary of Defense. It was comprised of three thousand federal employees and tens of thousands of defense contract personnel. Its primary mission was to develop, build, launch, and operate space reconnaissance systems and conduct intelligence related activities.

Villa stated, "Hi Todd! It's been quite a while since we've spoken. How are you?"

Smith replied, "Hey Miguel! It's been about a year. How are things at the DEA?"

Villa commented, "We are super busy, but that's no secret. Listen, we are involved in a major investigation involving the Azteca Cartel and their criminal associates. We anticipate several tons of cocaine to be shipped from Puerto Limon, Costa Rica, to Antwerp, Belgium, in the near future. We are going to place a transponder on it and we need your satellites to track it for us."

"We will be more than happy to do that," declared Smith. "Just send me the frequency the transponder will be using and leave the rest to us."

Villa responded, "Thank you, Todd. I will send you the information as soon as we hang up. I appreciate your support. Talk to you soon."

Meanwhile, on a secluded ranch ninety kilometers north of Guadalajara, Alarico and Samuel were coordinating a smuggling venture of half a ton of pure fentanyl into the U.S. through Matamoros. The lethal drug had been tableted four days earlier using a large pill press and then packaged in thick, blue plastic bags wrapped with long strips of tape. The fentanyl had previously been transported to the U.S. border in a single engine aircraft. It was now sitting at a tire warehouse guarded by Azteca Cartel gunmen. Alarico, using an encrypted Blackberry cell phone, called Lucio Fuentes whom he had handpicked to handle the logistics for smuggling the load of fentanyl across the border. Fuentes was extremely loyal to both Alarico and Samuel. He had been plucked out of extreme poverty by the two cartel leaders who made him a wealthy and respected man.

Alarico greeted his friend, "Lucio, how are you? Is everything ready on your end?"

"Si señor, everything is going well and we will cross this evening," Lucio retorted. "We paid one of the gringo customs agents and he will allow the load to pass without any problems. I let him know what would happen to him and his family, if he betrayed us. Once we cross, a cargo truck is waiting in Brownsville, Texas, which will transport the fentanyl to Chicago. Shortly after, you should see a lot money coming to you. The distributors there already have it sold. They told me you should prepare to send a ton a week because the addicts cannot get enough of it."

Alarico laughed and stated, "Pinches gringos, they have so much money they don't know what to do with it, so they kill themselves using drugs. Who are we to deny them that privilege? I also have to laugh at their stupid politicians who are legalizing marijuana. They will never take that market away from us since ours is more potent and we have more varieties. Not to mention our prices are much lower. Gringos locos. Each day, we steal a little bit more of their souls through our drugs. Forgive me for rambling on. Keep me informed on how it goes tonight."

Just as the sun began to hide in the western sky, a white, Toyota van drove up to one of the U.S. Customs inspection lanes in Brownsville. The uniformed inspector looked at the driver with a solemn look and with a wave of his hand let him pass. The van proceeded to a parking lot with a ten-foot fence topped with barbed wire. Thirteen large cargo trucks were parked inside. Two men in black hoodies were waiting. In less than fifteen minutes, the bags of fentanyl were transferred from the van into one of the trucks. Rustic southwestern furniture was then loaded to conceal the fentanyl.

The two hooded men jumped in the truck and began driving to Chicago, which was one thousand four hundred and thirty-five miles away. It would take slightly over twenty-one hours to get there. The men took turns driving and only stopped for gas and fast food. They drove through Shreveport, Little Rock, and Memphis. Finally, they arrived in Chicago and went to an auto repair shop in a predominantly Hispanic neighborhood and honked their horn. A large garage door opened slowly and they pulled in. Several men quickly began offloading the furniture until they got to the valuable cargo. They picked up the bags of fentanyl and held some of them high in the air in triumph.

Lucio called Alarico and declared, "Señor, the load is safe and we didn't encounter any problems. Everything ran smoothly according to plan."

"Gracias, Lucio," retorted Alarico. "You did a great job and I will give you a very large bonus for your efforts. We will be sending more and larger loads to Chicago in the next few weeks."

Alarico was pleased that he had decided to make Chicago one of his main distribution hubs. His decision was based on four things, transportation, ethnic makeup, size of the metro area, and gang culture. The city was within a day's drive of seventy percent of the nation's population and had six interstate highways crisscrossing the region, connecting east and west. Only California and Texas had more interstate miles. Chicago had six of the seven major railroads running through it. Alarico also saw an advantage in that Chicago's metro area had a large Hispanic immigrant population making it easy for Azteca Cartel operatives to blend in. The city was home to over seventy street gangs with over a hundred thousand members. They provided a ready-made distribution network for the cartel. Alarico was a visionary and strategic in that he knew there was more to just trafficking drugs. Like in any corporation, he selected geographical areas, which were more suitable and would generate maximum profits.

The half-ton of fentanyl was sold in less than two weeks making hundreds of millions of dollars for the cartel. Several weeks later, hundreds of users dropped dead from overdoses and many hospitals were inundated with emergency room episodes. It was always shocking what people were willing to put into their bodies. Even after close calls, they continued to poison themselves.

It was a hot, dusty day and Villa was at home watching the local news. The weatherman was giving his fifth forecast in less than twenty minutes. Villa was amazed reporters were unable to find enough noteworthy events in the entire state to cover a half-hour long newscast. The repetition was giving him a headache when his cell phone rang loudly to the theme of the godfather. It was Martinez in Costa Rica.

He stated, "Miguel, it looks like the cocaine is scheduled to arrive here in three days. We intercepted a call between Candelaria and Santos. The Colombian drug lord is personally coordinating the operation from Colombia. It's definitely a go. We have also identified the ship that will be used to transport it. It has been sitting at the dock with almost a full load of containers, but is obviously waiting for the load of cocaine. Tonight, Parra will sneak into the shipyard and attach the transponder."

"That is great news," quipped Villa. "I will give Voss in Belgium and Smith at the NRO a call just to give them a heads up. Good luck with the installation of the transponder tonight. Be very careful."

A tropical storm was coming in from the Atlantic and slamming into the eastern side of Costa Rica. As the winds and rain plummeted the area, Parra wearing black tactical gear climbed over a security fence and almost broke his ankle as he jumped to the other side. Slightly limping, he cautiously approached the huge container ship. He carefully placed the transponder just above the water line where it was virtually invisible. Parra, having accomplished his mission, climbed over the fence and hurried back to the hotel where he soaked his ankle in hot water for an hour.

Two days later, the agents, from a distance, watched as the ship finally headed into the open sea. An NROL-44 spy satellite orbiting thirty-six thousand kilometers above the earth immediately began tracking its movements as it moved eastward in the Atlantic Ocean. The satellite weighed more than five tons and had a huge parabolic antenna that unfolded to a diameter of more than a hundred meters in space.

The federal police in Belgium by now were intercepting hundreds of telephone conversations between Shehu and other organized crime networks throughout Europe. Most of these criminal groups were Shehu's clients and the others were his distributors. He proudly told them of the tons of cocaine he would soon have in his possession and wanted them to be prepared to distribute it quickly. The drug traffickers and law enforcement, like in a chess game, were laying out their strategies knowing there would only be one victor.

Almost a week later, Villa received a call from Smith who told him the ship they were tracking was a day away from Antwerp. He told Villa that it had not made any intermediary stops. As soon as they hung up, Villa called Voss and gave him the news. Voss stated they were more than ready and had several customs and federal police officers who would be responding to the port. He thanked Villa for all his support and would let him know how the operation turned out. It was now a matter of waiting for the ship to dock in Antwerp. Ideas were now swirling in the strategic mind of Villa whose mental gears were always in overdrive. He called Voss back.

Villa stated, "Listen, I have an idea. We have an opportunity to have a worldwide impact on the drug trade and I feel we need to take full advantage of the investigation we are currently conducting. Instead of arresting a few of the traffickers, we need to make the operation much more expansive. You obviously need to seize the ten tons of cocaine, but we should not arrest Shehu, if we can avoid it, so your wire intercept will continue and we can identify additional criminal groups in Europe as well as other members of his organization. We will not arrest Candelaria and let them believe the seizure was a fluke and not based on an ongoing investigation. Very soon, I will host an international planning meeting here in Albuquerque and bring high ranking police officials and prosecutors from all of the appropriate countries in Europe, Colombia, Costa Rica, and of course, Mexico. We will develop a strategy to dismantle as many networks as possible. The sharing of information between all of us will be critical."

"That is a great idea," commented Voss. "It will certainly put all of us in a better situation if we all work together and share information. I am all for it. Besides, I have heard so many wonderful things about New Mexico. Well, I will let you know how it goes tomorrow. Regards!"

The following day, the Palomino container ship docked in Antwerp. A total of ten containers were off-loaded by giant cranes at the dock and all were securely locked. The federal police were ready and had a massive tow truck. They attached a hook and chain to the first container and the door panel was popped open by the truck's powerful boom winch. Nothing! It was full of car parts. They did the same thing to the second one. Again nothing! It had boxes of avocados. They attached the hook and chain to the third one and the locking handle was yanked open violently. A mountain of kilogram packages of cocaine spilled out into the concrete.

While all this was going on, six men in a large truck showed up at the port cargo office stating they had come to pick up the container. Shehu was not among them. All of them were quickly taken into custody. According to plan, the Belgium media reported that a random search had resulted in the largest seizure of cocaine in the nation's history.

When he learned of the seizure, Shehu called Candelaria in Costa Rica in a panic and told him what had occurred. He also called numerous individuals throughout Europe to give them the bad news. A pen register installed by the federal police was identifying the numbers Shehu was calling and the numbers calling him. Intelligence analysts in Brussels were already pouring through dozens of numbers scattered all over the European continent.

Candelaria, after speaking with Shehu also began calling several numbers with consternation and the first one was to Alarico. The call was not answered and he tried again and again. He was successful on his fourth call.

Candelaria, his voice breaking up, stated, "Jefe, I have some bad news. They seized the load of cocaine in Belgium. Shehu called me and six of his men were arrested when they tried to pick up the container. It was apparently a random search by the authorities. Just horrible luck."

"Chingado, how is this possible?" screamed Alarico. "This is a big loss for us and we have to make it up soon. As you know, we have a lot of expenses maintaining our business. If we were not making most of our money on methamphetamine and fentanyl, the seizure could have proved to be fatal."

"Sorry to be the bearer of bad news," Candelaria replied meekly. "I will stay in contact with Shehu and hope he is not implicated in the seizure. These things are always a bitch."

"Please do that, and make sure the investigation they are conducting in Belgium doesn't come back on us," Alarico replied. "Hopefully, Shehu has covered his tracks well."

Two days after the large cocaine seizure, Villa invited U.S. Attorney Lillie Montoya to lunch to discuss the ongoing international investigation. They decided on a local Mexican restaurant specializing in soft shell tacos.

Montoya inquired, "So, how is your operation on the Azteca Cartel going? I heard of your ten-ton seizure in Belgium. That certainly must have had a substantial impact on the cartel."

"I am sure it caught their attention, but it is a very resilient transnational criminal organization," commented Villa. "The time will come when we will need your assistance in handing down indictments on members of the cartel. I am sure they will include many of the principal leaders."

"But of course, you don't want them melting into obscurity like butter on a hot tortilla. I will brief my staff on what to expect when your investigation comes to fruition," Montoya advised. "How soon do you anticipate things to start happening?"

Villa responded, "Hard to say, maybe three to four months if everything goes according to plan. I am having an operational planning conference here in Albuquerque in about two weeks with high-ranking police officials and prosecutors from several countries to coordinate the operation on the Azteca Cartel and other organized criminal groups associated with them. I would like for you to be there."

"Just let me know when and where and I will be there," Montoya replied. "It will be a major challenge since you will be dealing with the laws of so many countries or maybe even the lack thereof."

"Very true, but even so we can explore the possibility of indicting them in this country," Villa smiled. "Ok, enough about work. I am starved and they have the most incredible tacos here. The chef makes them just like my mother, the very best."

They had an enjoyable lunch and laughed at each other's jokes. Then it was back to work. There was a lot of planning and strategizing to do with little time to accomplish it all.

The next morning, Villa sent formal invitations to Germany, France, Italy, Spain, United Kingdom, Greece, Czech Republic, Belgium, Colombia, Costa Rica, and Mexico, to attend an operational planning strategy conference in Albuquerque. Its objective was to coordinate the dismantling of the Azteca Cartel and other multi-national criminal networks affiliated with it. The conference was scheduled to occur in two weeks. Within three days, all of the countries had responded and stated they would be sending their top police officials and prosecutors. Everything was set.

Things were now moving at a breathtaking speed. The DEA and IRS had already started coordinating with the Mexican Unidad de Inteligencia Financiera (Financial Intelligence Unit). It was an important administrative unit of Mexico's Secretariat of Finance and Public Credit responsible for detecting and preventing financial crimes such as money laundering and terrorist financing. Like most financial intelligence units, it was responsible for receiving and acting upon reports regarding suspicious financial transactions. They also analyzed financial data and trends. Of great significance, its main source of intelligence were the reports provided by the financial institutions throughout the country.

Romero, Holmes, along with Parra, Tanuz, Martinez, Quintana, Gil, Aguilera and Bert and Migel Flores had started to identify Azteca Cartel assets located primarily in Mexico through informants, and telephone intercepts of cartel members. The assets already identified included tens of millions of dollars in properties and bank accounts. More assets would undoubtedly be discovered as more time was spent mining the information on hand. The Financial Investigative Unit had also identified a large chain of high-end jewelry stores in Mexico City through suspect deposits at various banks. The owner of the stores was listed as Mercedes

Morales, a distant cousin of Alarico. A surveillance by Mexican authorities at the stores revealed they were selling very little merchandise, but yet depositing millions of dollars each week from alleged sales. The information being developed was quickly filling several large file cabinets in the office. IRS agent Romero led the team going over the reams of financial information and extracting valuable leads.

The objective was to generate a simultaneous strike in multiple countries against the drug trade worldwide, which was extremely complicated, but Villa was confident they could pull it off. The coordination would have to be laser focused and close communications between all countries would be the key to it all.

The time came for the planning session and all the representatives arrived and came prepared with files and information they had developed through time, some longer than others, but all exuded tremendous energy and enthusiasm. Villa had rented a large conference room at one of Albuquerque's best hotels. When everyone was seated and attentive, he opened the conference.

Villa, in a strong voice, remarked, "I would like to welcome all of you to the beautiful Land of Enchantment and truly thank you for making the long journey. Our struggle against transnational organized crime has to be a collective one. We must all unite and work together in order to effectively combat it. Drug trafficking does not respect borders or the rule of law.

Traffickers are a scourge, which corrupts democratic forms of government and foment horrific violence in order to poison our youth. Through the sharing of intelligence and evidence, I can guarantee we will be victorious. Today is a new dawn and the objective of this conference is to identify criminal groups that are directly tied to the Azteca Cartel throughout the world. We need to share pertinent information, which can be used in our respective countries. Subsequently, all of you will need to quickly initiate wire intercepts, execute search warrants, debrief existing and potential informants, conduct surveillance and use every investigative technique in your law enforcement arsenal. Each country represented here today has a great advantage in that you can initiate wire intercepts with great ease, unlike the U.S. During our conference, as you can see by the agenda, each country will be given the opportunity to present their capabilities and what they have, thus far, developed on drug trafficking networks working intricately with and supporting the Azteca Cartel."

Romero, an expert and very seasoned money laundering criminal investigator, with the IRS Criminal Investigation Division for over twenty-five years then spoke, "We also need to focus on the seizure of assets such as properties, businesses, bank accounts, which have been derived from drug trafficking and other related crimes. We must hurt them where they will feel it the most, their pocketbook. We have the ability to trace drug profits worldwide and will help you in this regard. We also have analytical models that we are willing to share with you in the development of your own group of financial investigators, which can work hand-in-hand with drug investigators. Given time, we can also provide instruction on the use of financial analytics that will assist you in building cases against major drug traffickers. We will teach you how to follow illicit money."

Montoya then stood at the podium and stated, "I have taken the opportunity to bring several of my prosecutors to meet with you and discuss prosecution strategies such as potential indictments in the U.S., which criminals greatly fear because it removes them from their criminal infrastructure and their ability to intimidate or bribe authorities. Our plan of action will require the use of extraditions and we have treaties with all of you, which allow us to do that. We stand firm and eager to work closely with all of you. As Mahatma Gandhi once said, "Non-cooperation with evil is as much a duty as is cooperation with good."

All of the countries provided eye-opening presentations on the work they had done and were doing on drug trafficking organizations in their countries and all the individuals they had already identified. Many gave extremely compelling Power Point enhanced speeches. On the second day, the police representatives worked closely with the various prosecutors and wrote down all of the information that was relevant and would be able use in their respective countries. General

Leonardo Gallego from Colombia was given the telephone number used by Santos, head of the Gulf Clan Cartel, to communicate with Candelaria. The powerful general advised he would begin intercepting the number once he returned to Bogota. This would be a significant step to possibly eliminating the major source of supply for cocaine to the Azteca Cartel.

On the third day of the conference, Villa advised that two command centers would be established, one for Europe, located in Brussels, and the other in Mexico City, for Latin America. Every country would dedicate at least one representative who would be responsible for receiving and sharing information on significant enforcement efforts. This would facilitate coordination and communication between all countries. Villa also advised he would make sure DEA Intelligence Analysts would be in each command center analyzing, collating, and rapidly disseminating intelligence reports on a daily basis. Villa stated it was important for all participating nations to pass their information from the past twenty-four hours each morning to the command centers depending on their time zones. He requested all representatives be in place at each command center within seven days. Villa designated April 14 as the date for the simultaneous operation to take place, which was two months away. He knew it was audacious, but had great confidence it could be done. Each country would comply as no one wanted to be seen as the weakest one in the pack. He stated the operation would be code named "Operation Hornet." Everyone was enthused and honored to be a part of a multi-national operation. They were ready to move forward.

That evening, Villa invited everyone to his home for a party. He hired a chef from one of the local restaurants to make fajitas along with beans, rice, and fresh guacamole. The famed Mexican singer/composer, Alberto Angel "El Cuervo" attended and sang some of his songs and everyone had a great time. Villa knew the function would cement friendships and create a strong bond, which was critically important. The following morning, everyone caught flights back to their respective countries and were ready to begin work on the operation. In seven days, the command centers were operational and running smoothly.

A huge, full moon lit up the night as a warm breeze moved through Tequila, Jalisco. The fifty thousand inhabitants of the small town were home having dinner. During the day, most of the men toiled in the large fields covered in spiked agave plants, which they harvested to make the best tequila in the world. Five kilometers from the town, Alarico and Samuel were meeting with some of their cartel leaders. The discussion centered on their revenues from all the illegal drugs they were exporting around the world.

Alarico advised, "We continue to increase our profits, especially with fentanyl and methamphetamine. The money we make from the other drugs are also climbing, but make no mistake our bread and butter are the synthetic drugs. We are making billions of dollars each year and cannot possibly launder all of it so we have started burying it in hermetically sealed plastic drums in different ranches."

Simon, a plump man with shoulder length hair, stated, "Did you hear that New Mexico just passed a bill legalizing marijuana so they can generate money for the economically deprived state? My primo called me and told me about it."

Alarico laughed and replied, "Yes, I heard about it in the news. The stupidity of politicians never ceases to amaze me. They play right into our hands. As I have always said, we will be the ones to reap more revenue than any state in the U.S. because we have more varieties of marijuana, better prices, and also much higher quality. We have been in this business for over half a century and they are just starting. Not all, but certainly a lot of marijuana smokers go on to harder drugs, which again is advantageous to us. I know that New Mexico relies on gas and oil for about forty percent of their revenue. You would think that in the past century, the politicians there would have come up with better ways of making money. Their vision truly ends at the tip of their noses. I recently heard one of their stupid legislators comment that marijuana could not be controlled so why not legalize it. Using that ignorant rationale, why not legalize murders since they have been around since biblical times.

Their legislators are nothing more than small tadpoles in a small puddle of water, a muddied one to be sure. Not that I care, but why do something so provocative since they are one of the states with the highest percentage of teenage drug abuse and crime. Worse, New Mexico is almost last, of all fifty states, in education. Pinche pendejos! They have placed a welcome mat and opened the door for us to partake of their financial banquet. Gracias, Nuevo Mexico!"

Samuel declared, "What kind of example are they setting for their children? They are also ushering in another era of big tobacco they fought so hard to eliminate. They will never be able to control their legal marijuana market despite all the phony rhetoric, but we will certainly be able to do so by something they can't generate and that is wholesale violence. Do these legislators who have been living in their little cocoons think they can outsmart us? It is like a wolf pitted against a mouse."

Everyone laughed out loud. They filled shot glasses with the best tequila money could buy. Someone yelled out, "Here is to the great state of New Mexico. Thank you for all your help."

By now the winds of destiny began to swirl that could alter the face of much of the world, and how it would play out would be decided by a higher power. The Azteca Cartel continued to sell enormous amounts of drugs around the world and bribe more officials to the point where Mexico was rapidly becoming a narco-state. On the other hand, Villa and police forces in many countries continued to gather evidence and work tirelessly day and night. It would soon come to a violent climax.

Villa, Bert and Migel Flores, Chris Quintana, Mike Parra, Ed Tanuz, Emmanuel Rodriguez, David Gil, Alvan Romero, Glenn Holmes, Lupe Martinez, and Davey Aguilera were poring over the intelligence reports from the command centers and coordinating every facet of the operation. There was also intense coordination with U.S. Attorney Montoya's office. No one was getting any rest, but the adrenaline rush kept them going and focused. The team had not only identified the chain of jewelry stores in Mexico belonging to the Azteca Cartel, but also several auto dealerships, which sold high-end luxury cars. Just the jewelry stores and dealerships were worth over a hundred million dollars. The Mexican Financial Intelligence Unit was working closely with Romero and Holmes and pursuing leads on other potential assets.

The Federal Police in Belgium were identifying a significant number of criminals from Shehu's calls. As the European countries identified more telephone numbers they were quickly intercepted. The number of phones being monitored now numbered in the hundreds. In Colombia, General Gallego and his men had seized over five tons of cocaine in separate operations from phone calls intercepted from Santos.

Three weeks before the scheduled takedown, Villa sent Parra, Tanuz, and Holmes, to Costa Rica to coordinate the final details of the planned multi-national operation. He sent Quintana, Rodriguez, and Gil to Brussels to do the same. Villa took Martinez, Romero, Bert and Migel Flores, and Aguilera with him to the command center in Mexico City.

Shortly after arriving, Villa and his team met with members of the Mexican Marines, National Guard, and the Financial Intelligence Unit. Everyone was preparing for the pending operation. Teams had been assembled to seize the jewelry stores, auto dealerships and assorted properties belonging to the Azteca Cartel. The marines also had teams tracking the movements of cartel members throughout the country, and had identified several clandestine laboratories producing methamphetamine and fentanyl in the states of Jalisco, Nayarit, Michoacán, and Aguascalientes. They were assisted by the newly formed National Guard. They expressed concern about not knowing the whereabouts of Alarico and Samuel, but were certain they were hiding in the state of Jalisco. Villa told them not to worry. The DEA had Samuel's phone number and through the use of technology it could be quickly triangulated every time his phone connected to a cell tower. It created a time-stamped record known as cell site location information, which determined his position with only a variance of eight feet. He took out his laptop and punched in Samuel's cell phone number and in seconds, it provided the coordinates of where he was at in northern Jalisco.

Villa commented, "We will continue to track Samuel's location and everyone knows he is always with Alarico. We need to use every second of the day to plan this operation meticulously. Prior planning prevents piss poor performance."

Romero stated, "I will work with the Financial Intelligence Unit on all of the asset seizures to ensure they can withstand legal scrutiny and are not later given back to the cartel."

Within days, Villa, his team, and the Mexican authorities created designated teams to arrest each member of the Azteca Cartel who had been identified and had strong evidence against them. Each team was given photos of their targets, to include lab sites.

The day before April 14, a massive amount of security forces moved into position in Europe, Mexico, and Latin America. Villa, Romero, Martinez, Bert and Migel Flores, Aguilera, and thirty-five Mexican Marines flew in four Sikorsky UH-60 Blackhawk helicopters, which had four blades and twin engines. They had a top speed of two hundred and ninety-four kilometers per hour. Each was equipped with deadly M134 mini-guns capable of firing six thousand rounds per minute. They landed several kilometers from the coordinates being shown for Samuel's phone. Villa spoke with the marine commander and advised him all of the Americans would walk to the location where they believed the cartel leaders were staying. He requested that fifteen of the marines accompany them. Villa took a marine radio with him and instructed the commander to launch their assault at daybreak so it would be a coordinated air and ground attack.

As the sun was starting to set, Villa used a military compass to guide them through ravines and wooded areas. The tall grass brushed heavily against their legs. One of the marines tripped over a rock and fell hard on his face, but quickly leaped back on his feet. They eventually came to a clearing and in the middle of it stood a rustic ranch house with over a dozen late model cars. Several guards were providing security and carried assault rifles. Most of them were dressed in blue jeans, cowboy boots and sombreros.

Villa posted a couple of lookouts while the rest of the team rested among the weeds and trees. It was a long night and very early in the morning everyone checked their weapons and began to crawl closer and quietly surround the house.

Two hours later, the loud thumping sound of helicopters approaching could be heard. As the Blackhawks got closer thunderous blasts of gunfire erupted from the traffickers and men began screaming as they ran trying to take cover. When the saw Villa's team nearby, the traffickers let loose a massive barrage of bullets. Villa knew similar things were happening or had already occurred in other parts of the world during the massive operation. He fired his Beretta .9mm and killed two men who ran towards him. Romero shot a man in the shoulder spinning him around as he fell to the ground. It was complete chaos. Suddenly, someone yelled from the house that they were surrendering. Weapons came flying out the door and stepping through the blinding glare of the sun, legendary trafficker, Alarico, appeared with his hands in the air. Samuel and several other men followed him. The marines used plastic flex cuffs to handcuff them. Just then a single gunshot rang out from a small hill behind the house. Villa felt as though he had been hit in the back with a sledgehammer. He felt something warm running down his body and touching it with his hand saw it was red, foamy blood. Just then he felt a sharp pain and his legs buckled. He fell hard, face first into the ground and could taste the bland, grainy dirt in his mouth. He turned on his side and the light from sky illuminated his face. He closed his eyes.

In Mexico, over five hundred members of the Azteca Cartel were arrested, to include Alarico and Samuel. Assets worth half a billion dollars were seized along with four tons of methamphetamine and a ton of fentanyl. Several drug labs were located and destroyed by setting them on fire.

In Costa Rica, Candelaria and Palomino were quietly arrested. Authorities seized the maritime shipping business and bank accounts belonging to Palomino.

General Gallego and the Colombian National Police arrested Santos and over a hundred members of the Gulf Clan Cartel. They had a shootout with numerous cartel members a hundred kilometers west of Barranquilla and lost two police officers. Eight traffickers were killed. A truck carrying eight tons of cocaine was intercepted and seized in the city of Medellin, Antioquia.

In Europe, the arrests totaled over a thousand and almost four hundred million in assets were seized. Several transnational criminal networks were dismantled and many countries continued with their efforts on several others. Shehu was arrested coming out of his residence. He was shocked when he was surrounded by ten members of the federal police.

The global operation showed the impact countries could have by working collectively and sharing information. Many of the European countries sent medals of honor to Alvan Romero, Lupe Martinez, Mike Parra, Ed Tanuz, Davey Aquilera, Bert Flores, Migel Flores, Emmanuel Rodriguez, David Gil, Glenn Holmes, Chris Quintana, and U.S. Attorney Montoya. Villa received his at a local hospital in Albuquerque where he was resting after his near-death experience. He was fortunate that a Mexican Marine medic skillfully stabilized him until he could be evacuated to the U.S. The bullet, which penetrated his back was removed and thankfully missed his spine by less than half an inch. Flowers and visitors flooded his room during his recuperation.

Two years later, Villa found out that Alarico and Samuel had escaped from the maximum-security penitentiary, Puente Grande, in Guadalajara. They had bribed all of the prison guards with millions of dollars to gain their freedom. The chase was back on.

ABOUT THE AUTHOR

Michael S. Vigil, born and raised in Española, New Mexico, earned his degree in Criminology at New Mexico State University where he graduated with Honors. He later joined the Drug Enforcement Administration and became one of its most highly decorated agents. He served in thirteen foreign and domestic posts and rose through the ranks to the highest levels of the Senior Executive Service. He was the Special Agent in Charge of the Caribbean and San Diego Divisions. He further served as the Chief of International Operations in charge of all DEA offices worldwide.

Mr. Vigil has received numerous awards during his elite career such as law enforcement's most prestigious recognition: The National Association of Police Organization's (NAPO) Top Cop award. This award is only given to ten law enforcement heroes each year from thousands of submissions nationwide.

Many foreign governments have honored Mr. Vigil for his extraordinary and courageous efforts in the violent struggle against transnational organized crime. He is the only

American to be conferred the honorary rank of General of the Afghan National Police by the country of Afghanistan. China bestowed him with the "Key to the City of Shanghai." The President of the Dominican Republic presented him with an Admiral's sword at an International Drug Enforcement Conference. He is mentioned in over twenty books and appears on worldwide documentaries, and popular television programs such as **Gangsters: America's Most Evil, The Rise and Fall of El Chapo, Manhunt: Kill or Capture, and NETFLIX'S Drug Lords.**

He is a contributor to CNN, MSNBC, NBC, ABC, CBS, Telemundo, Univision, Chinese Global Television, NPR, TRT, Al Jazeera, BBC, TV Azteca, El Financiero Bloomberg, FOX, NTN 24, Caracol Television, CNN Español, and dozens of internationally syndicated newspapers and radio stations. He is also a contributor to the highly regarded Cipher Brief.

His highly acclaimed memoir, **DEAL**, was released in 2014. **Metal Coffins: The Blood Alliance Cartel, Narco Queen, Land of Enchantment Cartel, and Afghan Warlord** are his four previous action fiction novels. Many of the scenarios, however, are derived from his extensive experience as an undercover agent.

He is the only American to have a corrido (ballad) made in his honor by Alberto Angel AKA El Cuervo, a famous recording artist and composer in Mexico.

Mr. Vigil was responsible for the largest and most successful operations in the DEA's history. The most significant one involved thirty-six countries in the Caribbean, Mexico, and Central and South America.

After the fall of the Taliban in Afghanistan, he designed and implemented Operation Containment consisting of twenty-five countries, to include China and Russia. Prior to this initiative, only a few kilograms of heroin were seized in the region. During the first year of Operation Containment over twenty-four tons were seized in this same region. The U.S. Congress continues to fund the highly successful initiative. He also developed regional intelligence centers allowing foreign countries to exchange information on transnational organized crime. The centers are now operational globally.

Mr. Vigil was one of the most intrepid and legendary undercover agents in the history of the DEA. He successfully infiltrated some of the most violent and dangerous cartels in the world.